What they're saying about
STEVE RASNIC TEM

"[Tem's] stories have the compression of poetry. He is able to create rapidly a mood of menace and revulsion."
—Publisher's Weekly

"No one has written so well of the inward spirit of the unwanted child since Shirley Jackson."
—Stephen King, Bram Stoker Award-winning author

"[Tem is] a rare treasure."
—Dan Simmons, Bram Stoker Award-winning author

"Steve Rasnic Tem is a school of writing unto himself."
—Joe Lansdale, Bram Stoker Award-winning author

"I've read a lot of stories by Steve Rasnic Tem and have never failed to be impressed by their extraordinary range and originality."
—Otto Penzler, Edgar Award-winning editor

"Lusciously grisly, creepy, and original, glimpses into the souls of people you would never want to meet. Tem actually scares me—hard to do—and I love it."
—Vicki Hendricks, Edgar Award-nominated author

"[Tem] valiantly goes to the bad places and shares his insights so you don't have to face head-on those same vicious struggles."
—Tom Piccirilli, Bram Stoker Award-winning author

"I've not only read Steve Rasnic Tem over the years I've also learned from him as both a writer and a human being. He's one of the true masters."
—Ed Gorman, Ellery Queen Award-winning author

ALSO FROM NEW PULP PRESS

A Death in Mexico, by Jonathan Woods

Hell on Church Street, by Jake Hinkson

Crime Factory: The First Shift, by various authors

badbadbad, by Jesús Ángel García

The Bastard Hand, by Heath Lowrance

The Science of Paul, by Aaron Philip Clark

21 Tales, by Dave Zeltserman

Flight to Darkness, by Gil Brewer

The Red Scarf, by Gil Brewer

A Choice of Nightmares, by Lynn Kostoff

As I Was Cutting, by L.V. Rautenbaumgrabner

Bad Juju, by Jonathan Woods

Rabid Child, by Pete Risley

The Disassembled Man, by Nate Flexer

While The Devil Waits, by Jackson Meeks

Almost Gone, by Stan Richards

The Butcher's Granddaughter, by Michael Lion

In Nine Kinds of Pain, by Leonard Fritz

UGLY BEHAVIOR

STEVE RASNIC TEM

A NEW PULP PRESS BOOK

First Printing, August 2012

ISBN-13: 978-0-9828436-9-7

ISBN-10: 0-9828436-9-0

Printed in the United States of America

Visit us on the web at www.newpulppress.com

Contents

UGLY BEHAVIOR

INTRODUCTION: THE DEPARTMENT OF UGLY STORIES

I'm not particularly known as a writer of violent stories. But ugly stories, tales about the terrible things we do to ourselves and to each other, have always accounted for a portion of my work. (And of course there are those who believe all tales of crime and horror—whether supernatural or not—are by definition "ugly" and do not care to read about these things. A collection such as *Ugly Behavior* would not be for them.) Both for those readers who appreciate this sort of thing, and for readers who would prefer not to encounter this other mode of mine, I've put all these ugly stories together into one box. It's that box under your bed, pushed all the way back against the wall, the one that takes some effort to get to, the one your momma doesn't know about (or at least, the one you like to think she doesn't know about).

As ubiquitous as that age-old reader's question, "Where do you get your ideas?" is that question specifically put to crime and horror writers, "Why do you want to write of such things?" or perhaps more to the point, "Why would you want to tell such an ugly story?"

In my case people often say, "But you look so peaceful . . . you seem so optimistic." People see this as a contradiction. In truth, I am an optimist. I believe wonderful things can come out of the most terrible events. I also believe life is hard enough for most people and we have no business making it even harder if that can be avoided. I believe we have a duty to each other to be as kind as possible. And I want my kids and grandkids to surround themselves with good and kind people.

I also believe the world is full of predators and the vilest kinds of monsters. People are capable of the ugliest behavior. For me, to ignore these things is to ignore the deadly snake in the room. We need to know what we're up against, so that we can really appreciate what it means to "behave honorably."

The other thing that sets these stories apart from the majority of my work is that no fantasy elements are involved. The terrors here are the daylight terrors of human interaction.

At times transcendence and transgression appear to be unexpectedly close neighbors. Most of us, I think, crave some sort of transcendence. We want to move from where we are in our lives to a better place. But when we cannot achieve that, some of us will choose transgression. Of course sometimes transgressing societal norms may be the only way to achieve some kind of social evolution. But we cannot always tell the difference between that positive action and its destructive counterpart. We become so eager to escape the limits of everyday life we are just satisfied that there's been any kind of movement at all.

—Steve Rasnic Tem, 2010

2 PM: THE REAL ESTATE AGENT ARRIVES

In the backyard, after the family moved away: blue chipped food bowl, worn-out dog collar, torn little boy shorts, Dinosaur T-shirt, rope, rusty can, child's mask lined with sand. In the corner the faint outline of a grave, dog leash lying like half a set of parentheses. Then you remember. The family had no pets.

SAGUARO NIGHT

My father used to say he loved the southwest because here it's obviously the landscape that matters and not the people. People who try to compete with their buildings, their roads, and their works are all just too pitiable, as if they were desperate for God's attention. "In the process they came damn near to ruining this country," he'd say. "I mean, look at Phoenix." Never mind that I liked Phoenix; both as child and daughter my opinion on the matter didn't count. If my brother had lived past the age of six his opinion might have had more weight, but I honestly doubt it, even though I've held onto the notion now and then as a convenient source of resentment.

Once or twice a year my father would drive me up to the Grand Canyon just to put me in touch with something "beyond man's power to alter." To me the Canyon was just this great big hole in the ground, but I knew better than to say that to my dad. Dad said he was glad he was a painter and not an architect in the face of such awe-inspiring vistas. This landscape, he said, required an artist already in sympathy with that world where human concerns were irrelevant.

My father was the perfect artist for that landscape. He had a "problem" with human beings, was the way he put it. Not a fear, exactly, but an obvious unease. Not exactly a hatred, or at least not a hatred he would admit to, but a profound distrust. If you look closely at his most famous painting, "Saguaro Night," you can see signs. Row after row of blackened saguaro lean forward as if marching toward a distant wrinkle of mountains. The sky behind and above all this is deep, inky, unfathomable. The painting seems simple enough at first glance, but then you start thinking why are the cacti so black? Has there been a fire? I always thought they looked as if they were suffering. Maybe they're not cacti after all? My father didn't paint them realistically, exactly, but in a style he called tormented expressionism. The lines are tortured, the shapes distressed, the colors despairing. No one really "likes" the painting, although it has fetched incredible prices over the last few years. I've heard that the last two owners couldn't bear to hang it in their homes. I'm told that once an old woman, a concentration camp survivor, burst into tears upon seeing it in a traveling exhibition of my father's work.

One cactus is not black—that small one in the background, on the edge of the right upper quadrant, a shimmering red-orange laid in with a few quick strokes, hardly formed, really. But so compelling. Some people say that's where the other cacti are leaning toward, their cactus deity. I'm not so sure about that, but I do know that's where the eye goes.

So my father's primary artistic inspiration was a distrust of human beings. Like any good daughter, I became his opposite. My weakness as an artist, and as a human being, is that I've trusted and loved people too much. My paintings, and my relationships, have been overwrought, sentimentalized, unrealistic affairs. Critics have pointed out superficial resemblances in our work, always to my detriment. Certainly I learned my technique from him, but I've always taken it too far—I lack his iron discipline. And we're both attracted, at least initially, to drunks and addicts. But after a year or so of passionate involvement, my father always leaves his unfortunate choices behind. He was with my mother a record two years, two months. I usually stay with my lovers until they ruin me.

And yet, strangely enough, for all this I always knew that my father both appreciated and loved me. I was always the only one.

My father had lived by himself on a small ranch outside Tucson for over twenty years when I came to stay with him the last few years of his life. I was running from yet another bad relationship. I suppose because this one had been so particularly bad, I ran to my father. Dad's relationships, also, had always been spectacularly bad. But he survived them, even thrived on these dramatic break-ups. He always appeared more content afterwards, and his paintings only improved. I decided this was yet another area where I could learn from his technique.

"So this young man, do you suppose he'll be following you here?"

"God, I hope not."

"There is no god, sweetheart," he corrected me quietly, matter-of-factly, as had always been his way. I had been watching him paint—he didn't mind; he said he'd just pretend I was yet another saguaro cactus—and I wondered at what he was working on. All his paintings those last few years started the same—he painted the blacks first, the endless sky, the mirroring ground. Much later more specific objects would appear, as if he'd shone a flashlight on them, or rubbed the night away just enough to reveal them. The beginning he made that day would evolve into the painting which became known as "Saguaro Night."

"Sometimes I forget, Daddy." He didn't say anything, but I could see his cheeks lifting slightly. I knew he was smiling, just a little. He was very lean, and the first signs of his illness were just beginning to show. His muscles moved with no secrecy beneath his skin.

"When you were little you asked me to paint a picture of God for you," he said. "I suppose if I stopped this painting right about now . . ." He added another brush of darkness to the canvas. "I guess I'd just about have him."

On impulse I hugged him from behind. I shocked myself—usually I didn't dare touch him while he was working—but he didn't pull away, and I didn't feel him stiffen at all. He just kept adding more of that endless night sky to the painting.

The summer was passing uneventfully. The days were beyond hot, and although he kept several ancient fans around, he refused to have anything to do with air conditioning. I didn't paint anything, even though he had set aside studio space for me in an annex to his own work room. I could feel his intense disapproval, but he never said anything. I couldn't imagine working in such heat, worse than anything I've ever experienced, but he was at it eight hours a day, seven days a week. After dusk he would fix us both some dinner—he never permitted me to cook—and afterwards he would sit in a rotting old chair on the edge of the desert twenty or so yards from the house, just watching the night sky that existed, I think, both outside and inside his head. He wasn't exactly unfriendly about it—he often invited me to join him, but I always declined. This was his, and besides, there was only one chair out there.

We never saw anyone except for a couple of old cowboys who came by now and then to do repairs to the house or the fences, and the boy from the local grocery in his battered green pickup. Each time I'd open the door to let the boy in with the supplies I'd be amazed at how wet he was, and how he seemed just a bit smaller than the last time, as if his brown skin were shrinking around him like the sheath over a fried sausage link. I stayed inside on days like that—the newspapers the grocery boy brought each time (just for me, of course), talked about windshields on parked cars exploding from the heat. I wrote lots of letters during that summer to old friends and boyfriends, but I didn't mail any of them. The letters were all alike, and like my father's paintings: all about the heat and the sky, and the dark that came without street lamps to lighten it.

But sometimes I'd start writing about the dark and the sky, and something from the newspaper would slip into the letter, almost without my noticing it. I suppose that shouldn't have been too surprising, since all there was to write about was the dark, the heat, and the sky, and whatever I read in the newspaper.

A lot of terrible things happened that summer, according to the papers (I had no reason to doubt them, but I'd never felt so isolated from other people's news as I did then so it was a little like reading about these events in a novel). Four girls, ten to eighteen, had been raped, strangled, and left out in the desert where the animals found them before their families did. A father had locked himself in the house with his three kids and then set fire to the place, while the mother sat wailing and screaming helplessly outside. A shoplifter had been chased from a downtown store where three cowboys caught him, beat him, then threw him out in front of a moving truck. The usual run of traffic accidents, bad enough in and of themselves, but then there was that especially hot Wednesday afternoon that a long distance truck driver "went strange" and plowed down the highway hitting everything and everyone he could. The final death toll on that one was twenty-eight, with a dozen more permanently disabled.

My father came up behind me while I was reading the story. I looked up at him and he said, "You want to know why."

I nodded.

He gazed out our back window at miles of desert with saguaro that seemed somehow too upright, and closer to the house than I remembered them. "It's just the sky," he said. "And the dark nights, those distant mountains, the heat. That's always been, I think, at the heart of it."

Tommy showed up at the ranch around the second week of August. "Hey, Babe. It's your sugar daddy!"

Sadly enough, the heart does go pitter patter at times like these. I remember seeing him there in a white dress shirt and tight jeans, leaning on the door jamb with one arm, his legs crossed to show off some rich leather cowboy boots. If I were younger I'd think that pitter patter meant true love. But I've come to realize that, at least for me, it was just the anxiety spawned by the attraction to someone bad for you. Of course my first thought was where did this New Jersey boy get those boots? Either he conned a woman at some bar to buy them for him, payment for services rendered, or he'd just stolen them outright. My second thought was how much he looked like James Dean standing there, and of course there was nothing accidental about that. He loved the movies as much as I did, and he knew how to duplicate a pose. I'd seen him do it in front of a hundred different mirrors.

"How'd you find me?"

"What? No 'Hi, how are you, it's great to see you, I'm glad you took the time to come all this way?' That's hurtful."

"We broke up, remember?"

"I know. It wasn't my idea, exactly, but I was there. Doesn't mean we can't still be friends. You know I'll always be there for you, babe. You're just that important." He stepped forward, his arms out.

"Tommy, no."

"Just a hug, girl. I swear, that's all." So I let him hug me. I didn't hug him back; not knowing what else to do, I patted his shoulder. "That's nice," he crooned. Cheesy, but I can't swear it didn't work.

I know I shouldn't have allowed the familiarity, the pretense that we'd ever been or would ever be anything approaching friends. I have no legitimate defense, but he was always one of those guys it was hard to give a final "no" to. It didn't matter what he did, I didn't want to hurt his feelings. It's crazy, when I think about it now, and hard to explain. It's just that when I was with him, especially after a long absence, it was hard to believe he wasn't exactly who he pretended to be, who I wanted him to be.

He let go of me and walked inside before I could bring myself to say anything. I was surprised to see him, after all, but I know I shouldn't have been. I made myself ask again, "How did you find me, Tommy?"

"You know, this place is great," he said, looking around, picking up things and putting them back down, touching the pictures on the walls. "Is this one of your old man's?" he asked, running his finger down the naked image of a woman in one of my dad's favorite oils, a present from an old friend who died when I was just a girl. It was a beautiful piece of art, and seeing Tommy's finger on the exposed paint sent me into a panic. But before I could say anything he removed his finger, examined it as if for rubbed-off color, and said, "No, of course not. It's too normal, right? But I can see why he likes it out here. It's small, but it's neat, and nobody to bother you, right? Nobody dropping by? You should have explained this place better, Babe. I always thought it was pretty lame, him living all alone out here like he was. But now I can see, I can appreciate why he'd like it so much. Hell, I'd like it here, too."

"Tommy, how did you find me?"

He looked at me, wiped the smile off with the back of his hand like it was something dirty. "Now don't be that way, Mary. I wanted to see you. I wanted to visit you. I care about you, Mary. Why don't you understand that?"

My alarm bells were going off, for all the good it did me now. Before when my Tommy alarms went off all I knew to do was run. But out here I didn't have any place to run to. All that was left was to try to mollify him. "It's just that we're pretty hard to find out here," I said. "Even when you know where you're going. Daddy wanted it that way."

"Daddy." He laughed. "I don't hear a lot of grown women using that word, Mary. That's a little girl's word. I know the old guy is a very smart man and all, a genius, right?" He didn't wait for an answer. "Well, I just got me some real good directions. That's all it takes, Mary, good directions. It's not like this place is top secret or anything. You know, it's not even that special, whatever your dad may say."

"You talked to my mother." No question, there. It was the only way I could think of that would have gotten him here.

"I told her I was trying to make things right with you again. She wanted to help out."

"You got her drunk, didn't you?"

"She's a very friendly lady, not stuck up like the rest of the family, who seem to think they're better than everybody else on the planet."

"Jesus, Tommy, you didn't sleep with her, did you? Tell me you didn't sleep with her!"

Tommy kept walking around the room, looking at things, touching things, as if he was doing inventory. He wasn't looking at me, and he was doing that thing with his mouth he always did, that thing that looked like a smile, but he always said it wasn't a smile, it was just an expression. "You know, I don't know what you want from me. You've never taken the time to really understand me."

"Mary, you didn't tell me we had company." I felt myself go rigid, holding back a wave of anxiety that threatened to overwhelm me. My father had never met any of my bad choices before. It was as if the two halves of my life were suddenly, dangerously colliding, and I was powerless to stop it.

I thought that if I were just a healthy person, a strong and mature woman, I could say, Dad, this is Tommy. He isn't supposed to be here. He's followed me out here from New Jersey and if he stays in character he's going to cause us a lot of trouble, because that's what he does. He's dangerous—I think you should call the local police immediately.

That's what I wanted to say, but knew I would not. In fact, just the thought of saying those things made me tremble. I thought my trembling might be noticeable, given the odd way my father was looking at me.

Instead, I told him, "Dad, this is . . . my old friend Tommy. Tommy, my dad." I kept thinking about something my dad once said. Something like, politeness doesn't get us what we need, sweetheart. In fact, worst come to worst, it might even get you killed.

"Pleased to meet you, sir!" Tommy was half-way across the

room, offering my father a handshake. I saw my father hesitate, glancing at Tommy's narrow, long-fingered hand as if it were a scorpion. Then he took it, his wide palm practically covering it, as if he were shielding me from it.

Tommy looked at my father's hand over his own, a glimmer of surprise showing in his face. Obviously my old man wasn't quite what he'd expected. He pulled his fingers out of Dad's grip. Then he grinned, forcing a recovery. "Anyway, it's a real honor. Mary's told me so much about you, I practically feel like I know you already."

Dad nodded. "I understand. It's odd, though, that she's never told me anything about you."

"Why, Mary, I'm surprised," Tommy said, exaggerating his expression. "You're not keeping us a secret are you?"

I couldn't believe this. Did he get away with this crap? Well, of course he did. He used to get away with it all the time with me.

My father gazed directly at me with that appraising look of his that had always made me so uncomfortable. And so angry. He could end this charade now, if he wanted to. He could get rid of Tommy just like that—I'd seen him do it with uninvited fans and unwelcome salesmen—and that's all Tommy was: my uninvited fan, my unwelcome salesman. My father had no patience with things interrupting his day, unless they were carefully planned interruptions. It had never been that easy for me, getting rid of what got in the way.

"Then you'll have to stay for dinner," my father said.

Of course it was a test, like hundreds of other tests he'd concocted for me since I was a little girl. But I wasn't a little girl anymore, and he had no business. The three of us shared an awkward meal of stew and biscuits during which my father asked simple, straightforward questions, and Tommy provided elaborate, self-aggrandizing answers, much more than was needed for the conversation at hand.

"So you think you might like to settle down around here?" he asked Tommy, but looking at me, measuring my reaction. I made myself lock eyes with him, attempting to show no emotional involvement whatsoever, and naturally, failing.

"Well, I'm seriously considering it, sir," Tommy said, his mouth full of biscuit. Then he looked up at my father with these big, brown, puppy-dog eyes, his "sincere" look, and I cringed. You can't seduce my father, you idiot, I thought. "I've always believed that change was good, you know? Without change, things would just stay the same all the time, and that can't be good, can it? Unless what you had before was so good you'd be a fool to change. You know what I'm getting at?"

My father stared at Tommy silently for a moment, then said, "Yes, Tommy. Yes, I believe I know exactly what you're 'getting at.'"

"I know you're a smart man, successful and all. I just want you to know how much I respect you, and of course, respect your daughter. I know she and I have had our differences of late, and I want you to know I realize that was completely my fault. I take full responsibility, and I intend to make up for every disrespectful thing I did in regards to her. Of course, she's a little stubborn." Tommy glanced at me, making a stupid little, insincere smile. It was an incredibly awkward moment. When no one reacted, Tommy went on. "And that's a good thing, a sign of character, is the way my saintly grandmother would have put it. I certainly wouldn't want to change that. I just wanted to ask you sir, as a man of the world, a great artist, a successful man, if you think there might be a place for one such as myself, out here in all this beautiful country? It's such a rare opportunity, my getting to meet such a great man as yourself, I hope you don't mind, I just couldn't pass up a chance to get your valuable advice."

My father turned and looked at me, smiled. He waited, obviously wanting me to say something, but I wasn't about to open my mouth. He turned back to Tommy. "I believe, Tommy," he said, "that there is a place, and a function, for everyone.

There's an old bunkhouse behind the house. It's not much, but it is shelter, and I've always found it, peaceful. Feel free to stay there until you find your own place, your own function." He looked at me again, not smiling. "My daughter will show you the way." I thought I was going to scream, but I didn't even open my mouth.

I remember walking fast through the weeds and cacti, angry, out of breath, hoping to discourage Tommy from saying anything. He stumbled at my heels, and that gave me great satisfaction. "Hey..." I ignored him.

I didn't know who I was angrier at: this creep Tommy, for coming here, playing his old numbers in a place where no one was going to be fooled by his playing, or my dad, punishing me for not taking a stand, treating me like a school girl in need of basic training. And, as much as I couldn't stand Tommy, I hated the way my father had played him—it felt like a direct insult to me. And it was so typical of my dad. When I was a kid I thought that kind of behavior meant he thought he was better than everybody else, and I hated him for it. It took years, but I finally saw that he had the utmost respect for honesty, integrity, hard work. He just had an unusual intolerance for everything else.

"Hey, wait!" Tommy grabbed me and twirled me around. "I came all this way, your dad likes me, for fuck's sake, he invited me to stay here, so why aren't you talkin' to me?"

I turned my face up, thinking to spit at him, and found myself swallowing the bitter taste because of the look in his eyes. Because somewhere along the way, between the time I had escaped him back east and now, he had changed, he had taken a turn for the worse.

He pressed his lips so hard against my mouth I could feel his teeth under the skin, hard and sharp and barely contained. "I love you, Mary," he growled from way down in his throat, "I really do."

I struggled, but I was too scared to struggle much. He held me tighter, firmer, and I couldn't breathe. He growled some more, from somewhere deeper than his throat, and inside the anger I could hear him crying. And I still don't quite understand why, but I kissed him back, even as I tried to push him away.

Before I left him that night, after showing him how to turn on the lantern, how to pump the water with the rusted old handle, where the extra blankets were, where my father stored the reading materials he'd have no use for, he called me from the ratty old bunk where we'd been lying together and said, "Your bedroom's out on the end, other end of the house from 'Daddy's.'" It wasn't a question.

Something about the languid, self-satisfied way he said it chilled me. "How did you know?"

"Oh, I wasn't gonna just waltz right in. That wouldn't be too smart, now would it? I've been here, three, almost four days."

"How?"

"He ain't that smart. Out here by yourself, you forget how to take care. I got a sleeproll, tucked over behind that little hill. Some food, some dusty old binoculars, that's all I needed. Didn't I tell you I used to be a Boy Scout? Merit badges and everything? I know how to handle myself in places like this."

"Oh. Right. I forgot."

"Point is, I don't have to stay out here all night. You leave your window open, I'll be there. That old man'll never know."

"That wouldn't be a good idea, Tommy."

"Let me worry about that, babe."

I walked a few more steps in silence, my eyes on the saguaro raising their arms in pain or surrender. In the dark they always gave me the creeps. "My window will be closed. And I've got a double lock."

"But I love yoooou," he crooned behind me, and laughed.

We didn't eat breakfast together out here on my father's ranch, we never had. He was usually in the studio before he was even all the way awake. He said he wanted "a brush in my hand before the last dream wears off." I'd learned to respect that, even though it sometimes annoyed me. Why were artists exempt from everyday human interaction? I remember thinking that if I ever became a successful artist I'd expect no special considerations. It's only been recently that I've been able to see the arrogance in my holier-than-thou attitude.

I heard a "thocking" sound coming from somewhere behind the house, followed by laughter, a soft, sick squeal. I didn't know what it was at first, but it made me scared and anxious almost immediately. I ran out the back screen door into the morning glare, shading my eyes until they adjusted, hearing the "thock" again, the squeal.

The first thing I saw when my eyes calmed down was Tommy in a stained T-shirt, ball cap, and torn cutoff jeans whacking at stones with an old croquet mallet, the remains of a set I'd seen lying out there in the sand (Like many artists I knew, my father had accumulated a massive amount of junk which he permitted to rust and rot wherever he left it. It seemed to be another one of those habits permitted artists, but which made you a slob if you were in any other occupation.) The mallet cracked and flew apart, Tommy cackled, grabbed another old mallet off the ground, and continued swinging at stones. I didn't realize what his target was until it squealed again.

I gazed out toward the collapsing bunkhouse, and there by the corner of the porch I saw the poor thing: an old Javelina, its eyes wide, with something wrong with its legs. It struggled to get off its side, but kept falling back down. Then another rock hit it, and it squealed again. I felt sick. "Tommy! Stop it!"

"Hey, Babe. Just trying to put it out of its misery. I didn't cripple it—I swear! Nasty old thing—I stepped off the porch this morning and it damned near took my foot off. What the hell is it, anyway?"

"Javelina. A feral pig, you asshole! Stop that—you don't put animals out of their misery by making them suffer!"

Tommy lifted the mallet menacingly with his thin, spindly arm. He'd always been embarrassed by how thin his arms were, no matter how much he worked out. I'm ashamed to say I laughed, seeing him waving the mallet like that. He was furious. "Don't talk to me like that, you bitch! I didn't know—you're the one lives in the fuckin' desert!"

Then I heard a series of overlapping, coughing barks from somewhere beyond the bunkhouse. The rest of the herd. I turned to run back into the house. I didn't much care what happened to Tommy after that.

The first rifle crack made me turn around. The old Javelina lay still, its head in ruins. The second shot went over the heads of the two Javelina coming around the bunkhouse, sending them scrambling back, barking furiously. Belatedly, Tommy hit the ground, the mallet waving over his head as if to protect himself.

My father strode over, rifle in one hand, reached down and grabbed Tommy by the long hair down his neck, pulled him straight up to his feet. He shook him furiously. Tommy's eyes were wide with shock. Then he scowled, opened his mouth, looked at the gun, snarled, "Off of me!"

"I'm giving you five minutes," my dad said, waving the rifle. "No discussion." Then he looked over his shoulder at me, the gun still pointed in Tommy's direction. For a second I thought he was going to kill Tommy, and I was somewhat surprised to find it was the idea of my father getting into trouble that frightened me—Tommy could, well, whatever happened to Tommy was very much his own doing. "Do you want to go with him?" Dad asked me.

"Daddy! Of course not!" I wailed, shocked, furious with his misjudgment, heart-broken that he had no idea who I really was.

Later that day my father lightly tapped on my bedroom door, and in a voice that might have been sad, although I wasn't really sure because I didn't know sad when it came contained in my father, he invited me to come out and help him bury the Javelina. I recognized it for what it was. My father almost never apologized, but when he did this was the form it took, an invitation to participate as in his own way he made his small attempt to right the world. We stood together quietly, lifting the heavy, foul-smelling creature onto one of the extra blankets from the bunkhouse, wrapped it, then transferred it into the grave he'd spent a couple of hours digging, because he wanted the dimensions just so, according to some inner school of spiritual geometry. Then we alternated scraping the dirt in, and on, and although no words had been spoken, he finished this funeral with a small bit of twisted wire welded to unidentifiable, cast-off bits, which he pushed into the ground where the hole had been.

Nothing more was said about the event, and nothing more was said of Tommy, as my father went back to his art and his regular routine, and I struggled during my time alone to find my own art and work out my own rhythm within the world.

Weeks passed as they did so often in the desert, as if they didn't pass at all, but lay around under that heavy burden of heat, unable to move. Food was eaten, the usual minimum number of maintenance chores were done, artwork accumulated, both in my father's studio and in the confines of my own room, where my father never came.

Once a season Dad took that long journey into the city for supplies, artistic and otherwise. He didn't like the trips—not that he said much in actual complaint, but his attitude was obvious. For weeks preceding the trip he was like a wounded old bear, cranky and snappish, forgetful, unable to find things, casting things about looking for what he'd lost and ignoring the damage he caused. To make it tolerable he'd usually stay with a local gallery owner/art critic and his wife, who appeared to be his only actual friends in the world. They would always throw some small dinner for him, inviting a few smart people who admired him and were unlikely to offend him. He was one of those artists who thrived on a certain minimum amount of attention, but who hated the magnifying glass of praise.

If that couple was not available for some reason Dad would just sleep somewhere in his truck. "I like my truck," was all he would say in response to my very real safety concerns.

Despite his dislike for the journey, however, once begun he was committed to it, and always stayed away at least a week, much longer than necessary for gathering supplies. "Might as well make it a research trip," he always replied to my questions about this seeming contradiction. What kind of research was involved I had no real idea—he'd take a camera along but I never saw the finished pictures.

On the day of his departure the weather seemed to be turning cooler, with occasional streaks of rain like mist sprayed on a hot iron. Unexpected clouds would roll in over the desert, and although most of the time nothing came out of them, they did serve to cool things down a bit. During the dry afternoons I still heard the rattlers, the occasional complaint of some Javelina, scattered insect sound, and now something new, that buzz and whistle of toads over in the mesquite grass which gradually became something harsher, louder, a call that sounded a little like bleating sheep.

My father had been gone several days when I found myself wide awake one night, hearing a sound like a screech, like something electrical, like something coming apart at the seams. I sat up. Moonlight brought the shadows of distant saguaro close, walking my way, nowhere else to go. What did they want from me? What did they expect? I just do the best I can, I remember thinking, half asleep. I slipped out of bed, padded across the floor and gazed out the window. Wind whipped through the tall grass, brushing through the scrub, charging the night. About ten yards away, where the long ranch house bent to form my father's studio, jagged shadows danced in the window. Something gleamed, fell, rose again. I don't remember now if I suspected anything specific. I do remember the overwhelming panic I felt, the sense of impending doom. I ran out of my room, down the hall, full of charge, electrified, for some reason suddenly thinking that birds must have gotten into my father's studio and were now flying around in there, doing damage.

But, bursting through the door, looking around the ceiling, I found no sign of the unwelcome birds, just the arm flailing, making that rip, with exhausted, crying, out of breath sounds, like running, like rape. Then Tommy's face appeared around the edge of the canvas, that latest painting, still on my father's easel, unfinished. He grabbed it, brought the edge of the frame down on the floor, raised the knife again, and I just ran, arms waving, charged right into him, screaming, "No!" and "Don't!" and felt the knife go into my face like something hot and impossible, following the jaw line, peeling me away from myself.

When I went down on the floor I got a better look at the painting, the saguaro, shadowed, dark and lost, against the night, half-done, blood on the unpainted portions of the canvas, and yet, still, beautiful. So beautiful, such was my father's talent.

During those several weeks in the hospital my father never left my side. Investigators from the Arizona State Police came by several times, asked me a few questions, but for the most part consulted with Dad quietly in the hall. They might not know his art, but they knew he was famous, which to them, I suppose, meant he merited special attention. Or maybe it was because I was a girl disfigured by a crazy ex-boyfriend. I don't know, but everyone was solicitous, which I didn't mind.

I wouldn't have minded if Dad had gone home for awhile, though. Having him around twenty-four-seven, worrying about what he was thinking, was a bit much to bear. And the way he talked about the "incident," I could hardly stand it.

"They say he waited in the hills until he saw the truck leave. I don't understand it—I searched the area thoroughly after I kicked him off the property."

"You did? You never told me."

"I didn't want to worry you. But given his character, I thought he might stick around, plot revenge. Cowards, they always seek revenge."

"I wish you had told me."

"Maybe, maybe I should have. But I searched those hills, and beyond, thoroughly. I can't figure out how I missed him."

It was his way of taking responsibility, of expressing his sorrow, I knew. But it aggravated me how he'd turned this terrible thing that had happened to me into a puzzle that not only he hadn't solved, but that he might have prevented. My dad had god forbid made a mistake. "It's over," I said. "It's past. Do they know where he his now? Did you call Mom?"

He blanched. "The police called her, warned her. She should have come to visit you. I don't want to see her, of course, but she's your mother."

"I don't want to see her, either, Dad. I just thought she should be warned, in case he shows up at her house."

"They alerted the local police out there, and the state police in between. They're pretty sure, they think, he's left the state."

"That's good." We sat there in silence, neither one of us comfortable talking about it, but wanting to behave normally, and not knowing what normal behavior really meant. "Your paintings," I began, because I'd been thinking about them. To be honest, it was the first thing I thought of when I regained consciousness. "You said you could fix them?"

"They're going to be fine. They're going to be…" He looked at me, obviously excited, apologetic about being excited, "better, actually. Better than before. I've worked it out in my head. Applying additional canvas to the back for the repair, but beyond that—I was having a compositional problem with 'Saguaro Night.' The damage actually suggested a solution. It's going to be better, much more interesting."

Perhaps it was unkind of me, but for a moment I thought he was trying to suggest I was going to be much more interesting as well.

I don't know what more I can say with any certainty about those days. It was such a long time ago. Tommy was never seen again. Dad and I returned to the ranch. Dad continued to paint, in fact creating much of the work he is most famous for, beginning with the re-worked and completed "Saguaro Night."

I discovered my own vision, if you can call it that. With all the saguaro, the low-lying mesas, damaged landscapes, the dark skies, the feral pigs and other creatures, people have pointed out quite correctly that my vision owes much to my dad's. And after years of living here in the desert, so do my attitudes.

I was no beauty, before. When I look back I think the major thing attracting men to me had been my lack of standards. The scar along my jaw isn't so terrible—in fact from most angles it's barely noticeable. But what my father had so awkwardly implied, that it might make my face more interesting, turned out to be mostly true, I think. So I keep my chin raised higher than normal just to show it off. I've even been known to use makeup to highlight its shape, the aesthetic beauty of its line.

Dad died in 1984, his heart disease catching up to him one afternoon in front of his easel. I didn't find him until the next day—when he didn't show up for dinner I just assumed he was too involved in a painting to stop. I wasn't supposed to disturb him, even if he went missing. That was the rule, the artist's special rule. Unlike a normal person, he didn't have to show up for dinner. It's possible I could have helped him if I'd found him in time. I don't know; who's to say?

The first major retrospective was held in 1989. I was there, introducing many of the paintings. They gave me a show on the side as compensation. It worked out for me; I'm not sure I'd have a career today if not for that show.

It was the first time more than a handful of people had seen the completed "Saguaro Night." It created quite a stir. I showed them where the damage had been, and how the repair and subsequent paint-over had created a fracture line that led the eye through the marching saguaro and to the lone red figure on the other side. Although clearly embarrassed, a couple of people timidly offered the observation that that fracture line was reminiscent of my jaw line scar. Bullshit, of course—people see what they want to see.

"The magic, Mary, comes in how sometimes only a few tentative brush strokes of the right color, in the right position within the composition, make the painting what it is."

I hear that advice of my father's, and other bits of aesthetic lore, every time I stand in front of a canvas. And in my father's work, no painting bears the truth of that advice better than "Saguaro Night," and the few brushstrokes making that running, burning figure.

Those first few months out of the hospital I painted constantly, rarely taking time to eat or sleep, it seemed, rarely seeing my father, who was busy with his own creative firestorm, working on "Saguaro Night," and other, similarly dark paintings. Occasionally he invited me into his studio to see the progress he'd made on the painting. This was unheard of for him, and showed, I think, how sorry he was for what had happened. Additional evidence of this sorrow came in the form of late night rants to no one, drinking and stumbling around outside, wandering off into the hills. Screaming and cursing. Sometimes in the morning I'd find him stinking and out of it, lying in front of the door, and I'd drag him in. We never spoke of that. It became just another part of his artistic process, a stage in his "research," and therefore off-limits to conversation.

There was no red figure in the painting for the longest time. Then there came that night when the Javelina herd barked and squealed and just generally went crazy. And in the distance I heard my father screaming back at them. And in the distance I heard more screaming. And I looked out there into the dark Sonoran desert night and saw that he had built a fire out there. He had set fire to a saguaro, which raised its spindly arms in agony and tried to run away.

I'm not sure when he returned, but I heard him working in his studio all day, and he slept most of the next day, and the day after. That's when I slipped into his studio and saw that the red, running figure had been added, and that now the painting was complete.

On that second day of his sleep I saw the birds circling

a distant spot of desert. Remembering what we did for the Javelina, that poor dumb pig, I grabbed a shovel and headed in that direction. But I did not want my father's help, preferring to leave him to his dreams.

IN HIS IMAGE

"We wear the mask that grins and lies,
It hides our cheeks and shades our eyes."
— Paul Laurence Dunbar

Something iffy had slipped into his face. Of course it was probably just a matter of looking too closely. An occupational hazard—K.T. was always looking at things a little too closely. Couldn't see the forest—actually hadn't seen a forest in years. Couldn't see a face for all its pixels. He stared into the mirror, ran one finger down his skin from right eye to lower cheek, fascinated by the way the skin tones changed, the crinkles vanishing then reforming, new lines appearing, and everything just taking a few seconds too long to spring back into shape. A loss of elasticity, a decrease in flexibility. Signs of age as sure as the whitening of his scraggly beard hair and the bluing of the flesh under the eyes. A mask, wasn't it? K.T.'s old-man mask. Sometimes he considered shaving the beard and getting some sort of tribal tattoo across the lips and around the chin to replace it, maybe make the dark under the eyes a permanent, deeper mark. Something bold to mask his age. But he suspected that much tattoo on facial skin would be a painful process, and he didn't have the time anyway.

Instead he threw cold water on his face and turned away from the mirror. He didn't think many people liked what they saw in the mirror. Always this discrepancy between the face they imagined and what appeared on the screen. Like listening to your voice on tape: the words and the particular pattern of speech might be yours, but the voice wasn't yours at all. You sounded better, you looked better, in your head.

Except media types, actors, announcers. They spent their lives making the face and the voice match what they imagined, what someone else imagined, what they read in the script. K.T. figured he of all people should envy such control, but he didn't. There was comfort in the discrepancy between image and substance. Rightly or wrongly it suggested depth of character.

In any case, nothing to have an anxiety attack over. His favorite saying of late, he'd posted it at the top of his web site. Of course people who were compelled to remind you there was nothing to be anxious about often suffered from raging anxieties. He could feel the nerves playing with the muscles of his face like spider hairs. Damn, but he was a mess. Nothing to worry about. No big deal. The face was a mask and the mask was just a few cells deep, nothing more than a thin layer of electrons.

He made his way back to the screen, fatigue causing him to bump into things, sending stacks of old magazines tumbling onto discarded pizza boxes, stray clothing, unopened mail. He hardly noticed. He owed a new client a picture by midnight, and one of his few prides was that he never missed a deadline.

The assignment was another creepy one—he seemed to be getting a lot of those lately. A drawback of advertising on, doing most of your business through the web. Photo Manipulations Inc. There was always some fool wanting him to graft a young starlet's head onto a naked body, but that was more idiotic than creepy. He'd accept their credit card, though—who was he to say? They were just images, after all. They couldn't really hurt anybody.

But fellows like this new client—and they were almost always male, very few women appearing to need his services—what they wanted couldn't exactly be called pornographic, he supposed, but pondering the whys and wherefores of their requests to any degree always filled him with unease. The best he could do was lose himself in the technical aspects, leave the philosophizing to the alternative news groups. Wet images, dry images, women covered head to toe in a stew of nameless food items. Everyone seemed to have a special interest.

But it was all just a shim of electrons, a thin peel of a mask. Nobody died, they just got older, more set in their ways.

The new client had sent him a snapshot of a young boy, six, maybe seven, a little stocky, reddish hair, his back turned to the camera but his face twisted around to see who was behind him. Smart kid. It pays to know who's behind you. Only a hint of anxiety in the kid's expression but still plainly there, especially at the higher magnifications.

The other photo the client sent was that of a fat sow suckling her young on a bed of straw and gray, lumpy mud. K.T.'s assignment was to replace the sow's head with that of the young boy.

What K.T. was being paid for, of course, was to make it look good. It wasn't supposed to look as if someone had grafted a boy's head onto a hog's body. Skin tones and textures had to match, color blends had to be seamless. There had to be some hog in the boy and some boy in the hog. Despite your good sense, you had to believe your eyes. You had to believe that a creature such as this in fact existed.

He was almost done with the project, and even though he'd been staring at the image constantly over the last day or so, seen it even in his dreams, he still couldn't stand to look at it. So he looked at the picture and yet he didn't look at the picture. He looked at pixels, he manipulated bits and bits of bits, but he could not bring himself to look at this picture.

He had performed one additional manipulation, unasked-for, but which he knew from experience the client would want, even though he might not have the right words to ask for it.

K.T. had tweaked the areas around the eyes and the mouth to make the boy's anxiety more pronounced. No additional charge. A boy sow down in the mud, suckling his young. Completed. He didn't know what the client would do with such an image. He didn't want to know. He emailed a low-resolution sample, let the guy know how to download the higher quality version from K.T.'s site.

The rest of the evening K.T. worked on his web site, scanning images from magazines and newspapers, adding elements to aspects of his own face already in electronic storage. His web pages contained samples and descriptions of his business, price lists and submission information, but the deeper you went into the site the more personal it became, until finally you arrived at K.T.'s personal newsletter, Mews, and a gallery of images he'd created, including many self-portraits. He'd tried to explain in several different ways in the newsletter that the multitude of self-portraits on the site was not evidence of some runaway narcissism, but simply to avoid the emotional and legal complications inherent when you manipulated the faces of other people without their permission.

The title Mews had been a spur-of-the-moment invention, risking silliness in its multiple meanings. He lived in a complex called Dogwood Mews, meant to emulate an old English neighborhood with its facing townhouses and cobbled courtyard, the dogwood at its center in fact a sculpture of a tree out of wire and fibrewood and plastic laminates, the woodgrain a photographic image bonded to melamine. There were also word plays: "News" which he watched constantly but never seemed to believe or understand, the muse of inspiration of which he appeared to have very little these days, the musings of solitude which he had in plentiful supply, and finally the mews of complaint, the pitiful whining of a homeless or tortured cat, scratching and puking at the door. He'd originally included an image of a tortured cat as part of the masthead, which had outraged some so much he'd finally removed it. He kept explaining in his emails to these cat fanciers that the image had been manufactured, that he tortured images not animals, but many didn't seem to believe.

Most who bothered delving into these deep recesses of his site were more interested in his self-portraits than animal rights issues, however. Here his image suffered skinning, marring, evisceration, zombification, pixilation, posterizing, inversion, hue saturation, spherization, castration, immolation, all the tortures of the damned, and yet the only fallout for his physical being appeared to be intensifying fatigue.

Sometimes he recounted for his readers/viewers the steps involved in creating such personal disaster, but most of the time he was content to let them view the images without the technical background. People made assumptions about him on the basis of these images and sent him offers of aid both financial and psychological, long confessions, virulent diatribes, veiled threats, and more than one marriage proposal. He posted several commentaries suggesting that perhaps they interpreted too much, that an image took on a life all its own once manipulated, divorced from its original source, it's all just electrons, folks, charged particles and vapor-thin appearances and cosmic dust, but the outpouring had showed no signs of a decrease.

He had a second, larger monitor rigged up next to his first. After transferring some of his self-portraits to video, he would display them here, now playing twenty-four hours a day. This permitted exact-size images of his distorted head he might observe while working, talk to, stare at eye-to-eye. Disconcerting sometimes, especially if any animation was involved. The mouth dissolving into a smile full of bone, eyes full of charged desperation in confrontation with the creator.

This, perhaps, was what had sparked his increased use of the bathroom mirror. Something to touch base with periodically, an anchor, even if K.T. didn't always like what he saw there.

Suddenly he could feel a razor-thin line of anxiety forming at the right corner of his mouth. It stretched across his chin and hooked into his jaw. He scrambled out of his chair and ran into the bathroom. Stacks of images flowing out over the rug, opened envelopes containing uncashed checks. A wicker basket full of unanswered bills on the floor next to the toilet. He wondered briefly if they might cancel each other out. A sour strain of body odor and spoiled food, but buried too far under glossy magazine layouts to do anything about. No one knew where all the bodies were buried, despite their claims. Children were killed everyday over the internet and no one lifted more than a mouse-clicking finger. Children's faces stolen and peeled away, leaving their bodies awash in a sea of red electrons.

In the mirror: his face soaked in cold sweat, fluorescent highlights in the whites of his eyes. He pushed closer to the glass and examined his face for rips: a nervous twitch by the mouth, a deep crease, but no trace of blood. He breathed a trembling sigh of relief. He looked terrible, but it was just an image, and he of all people knew that images could be edited.

A thunder of surround sound. The walls appeared to shake around him, his fingers twitching in accompaniment as if typing in changes. A couple of deep breaths to calm himself—he figured it was all a problem of sleep deprivation; he got obsessed with the work sometimes and simply couldn't be bothered with sleep—but his breath tasted of dank places and bad food and would not heal him.

A beating at the door. The infrequent visitor. He slipped back into the living room, performing a rapid survey of cleaning and straightening possibilities, and finding none elected to open the door anyway, not wanting the beating to continue a second longer. A pregnant woman stood in his doorway, weaving and drunk. He vaguely recognized her as a neighbor from across the way, despite the fact that a purple half-mask with plumes of ascending feathers covered the upper part of her face.

"So I heard you typing. Most nights I walk by I can hear you typing. Are you an all night typer or something?"

The mouth that said these words was unmasked, but outlined in a bright red lipstick that made it much more disconcerting than the half-mask above. The lipstick had an aging effect. Even with the mask he could tell the woman could be no older than thirty. The lipstick mouth added decades. It waited patiently for an answer. "Well . . . I work with computers," he said. "I hit the keys pretty hard sometimes."

"I wouldn't know much about that stuff. But the thing is . . . my boyfriend's gone out again, and I'm scared being all by myself. Can I just wait here 'til he gets home?"

K.T. heard the words, but he really had no idea what she was saying. It might as well have been a foreign language. He couldn't remember the last time he'd spoken in person to a woman other than a checkout clerk. He wasn't sure he'd ever spoken to a pregnant woman. So he did what he always did when someone spoke to him in a foreign language. He tried to be the polite American. He nodded his head a great deal and smiled, even when she walked into the room. He didn't ask why she was wearing a Halloween mask in the middle of July; it would seem seriously rude to show any curiosity at all.

"Oh, look here. All these books and magazines and things to read. You must be a smart guy. I like to read, especially comic books. You like comic books?"

K.T. was pleased to hear a question he could answer. "Oh, yeah. I really love comic books."

"Do you have any Silver Surfer I could read?"

"Well, sure. Grab yourself a chair. I'll find you a Silver Surfer." He said it as if he were offering her a drink, and wondered if he should offer her a drink. But he wasn't sure what he had. He made his way into the kitchen, pausing now and then to lift up a stack of magazines as if looking for the comic, but knowing very well where the comics were. He felt so inordinately pleased to have the exact comic she wanted to read—what were the odds of that?—that he'd forgotten there were no empty chairs in the room. With the exception of his computer chair they were all piled high with boxes of clippings, and magazines waiting to be clipped.

He glanced over nervously to see her sitting on the edge of his bed, which he kept pretty much near the center of the room so that he might drop onto it periodically if he needed a computer break. He hadn't made it up or changed the sheets in a very long time, and seeing it now—and when you saw things through a veil of anxiety sometimes it was like seeing them for the very first time—he could see the yellow-brown pattern his body had etched into the bottom sheet. He could detect where his arms and legs had been, and his head, lighter patterns there like a facial topography. A clear spot like a mouth open in a faded mask. Instantly thought Shroud of Turin, and with that detected a small trace of blood near one corner of the image—he remembered a cut foot—but of course it looked like something more deliberate now. This gave him the idea for a sequence of images he might construct for his web site: portraits of people but with the people peeled away, only their shadows, and the shadows of their shadows, remaining. He would play with these remaining shadows, emphasizing and distorting them, perhaps distorting the objects they fell on, creating transformations wherever they touched. It would be a hopeful sequence in its way, advancing the idea that we could be effectual, even when fading into obscurity and oblivion.

There was orange juice in the refrigerator that smelled relatively fresh. He thought that would be the safest thing he could offer her.

From the other room, "Hope you don't mind my sitting on your bed?"

What was he supposed to say to a question like that? Was she coming on to him? "Oh . . . fine. Wherever you feel comfortable."

He gave her the juice when he came back in, feeling just a little alarmed that she hadn't yet bothered to remove the mask. As if reading his mind she said, "Tommy gave me this mask last week. He says I have to wear it all the time when he's not there. I don't mind it too much, but it makes it a little hard to see my TV programs with it on. I have to tilt my head some, make sure the eyeholes line up, but sometimes it slips. I tried putting a big old rubber band around my head to hold it in place, but it gave me a headache."

K.T. found a copy of the Silver Surfer and handed it to her with the juice. He didn't like the way she was leaning back into the bed, her skirt riding up. And her belly looked even larger in this posture, rising up off her spine like an explosion. "Maybe you could take it off for a few minutes, at least until you're done with your juice."

"Oh, I couldn't do that. He'd have himself a fit. And he doesn't even look like himself when he's mad."

"Most of us don't, I guess. I mean, the skin on our faces is so thin, really. Any strong emotion is going to move the features around in some significant way."

"You're a smart man," she said, as if just deciding. "I bet you wouldn't make your girlfriend wear a mask even after Halloween. That's just ignorant."

"Well, it is a little unusual."

"I bet you treat your girlfriend right, don't you?" Her voice lightly slurred the words. "I bet you appreciate her for what she is." Before he could confirm or deny she flipped open the comic. "I really like the Silver Surfer. His face is like he's got a mask on, but it isn't a mask, not really."

"His face is like what they call a 'neutral mask,'" K.T. replied, eager to offer some obscurity now that his intelligence had been established. "It's a mask without any details, molded to the face like a hardened layer of skin."

She looked up then. Even with the mask on she appeared slightly dazed by the concept. "Well, I don't think it's a mask," she finally said. "I think he's kind of a good looking man." She picked up the comic and started reading. "You know you can go back to your work. I'll just sit here reading quiet until Tommy gets home."

The polite thing would have been to tell her he was done for the evening, then try to entertain her, ask her about her life, somehow ask her about what kind of man this Tommy was to make her wear the silly mask, but K.T. didn't know how to do polite. Besides, he was anxious to get back into his work—this was the most he'd talked to a live person in weeks and he had no idea if he was doing it correctly or not—and she'd just given him the easy out.

A distorted image of him stared out from his second monitor. In some ways it looked better than him, a retouch job with straighter nose, stronger chin, and firmer eyes. His eyes looked so watery and unsure, as if always on the verge of tears. He couldn't remember having made this particular self-portrait, but then again he had made so many.

He logged on, picked up his email (the client was more than pleased with the sow child), then went over to his web site.

At first he thought a hacker had gotten in. There appeared to be alterations in all of the images in his gallery. Some fleshtones had deteriorated, leaving faces with a green or grayish cast. Pixels had floated out of place, outlines blurred. But not really enough damage, he thought, for it to be actual sabotage. Maybe a problem with his graphics card. Or maybe a problem with his own eyes. Fatigue can distort the curvature of the lens and . . .

Something iffy had crept into the eyes of his self-portraits. Or crept out of. The flatness, the deadness was gone. The eyes, even in heads of pain, watched him.

"So you think I'm pretty?"

He'd been so zoned he'd forgotten she was there. He looked up at her, the young pregnant lady stretched out on her back on his bed full of signs and indications, mask obscuring the upper part of her face, bright red lipstick alerting him to where her mouth would be if he wanted to come over and try it out. "Excuse me?"

"I said, do you think I'm pretty?"

Definitely someone else's life. But he could play along—he'd watched enough television, gone to enough movies. "Well, yes. Of course," he said, delivering his line.

"Why, thank you." She cozied back into one of his hair oil-spotted pillows. "I don't get too many compliments anymore."

Her pleasure saddened him. For the first time he noticed how faded her simple cotton dress appeared. The spots, the worn places. "Everyone needs a compliment now and then." His eyes went back to the monitor. One by one his images were slipping off the sides of the screen, leaving video noise in their wake.

"Well, ain't that the truth. Even if you know you're ugly, and you know the other person is lying through his teeth just to get into your panties, well, you still like to hear that sweet stuff."

He could feel his face flush, tried to will it another color, perhaps just a hint of Caribbean tan. "I don't even think I believe in ugly anymore," he said. "It's all just one image set up against another. Some looks get marketed better, that's all. Sometimes you can change your marketing, and sometimes you can't. That's the scary part, I think. You feel so damn helpless about it all. All these damn images of beauty and success and happiness that'll fit inside a frame and stay there while you look at it, admire it, covet it. And if you aren't careful, it all becomes this minefield that nobody ever gets out of alive. That image is a killer—it's got all our need and fear balled up in one place—it's a terrible thing and yet even the smartest of us think that's all we are."

Her head was bobbing, but it was because she was looking around at the clutter of his living room. He wasn't sure at what point he must have lost her; he hadn't been paying that close attention. But lost her he had.

Suddenly he felt acutely embarrassed for the way he lived. The place was like some skid-row trash heap and he was just the fly that landed there. He looked down at his stained T-shirt and shorts. He hadn't even been aware what he'd been wearing when she came to his door. He could've taken a bathroom break and washed and changed his clothes before coming back out but it seemed too late for that now. She could see how he lived and what he'd become.

"That's a real nice sports jacket," she said, oblivious to his musings. "Did it cost a lot? I bet it did and I bet you make good money doing this typing thing."

He tried to follow her line of sight, saw the sports jacket sprawled across an end-table where he'd thrown it after the last disastrous job interview. He could have done the job, of course—he never applied for any job he couldn't do—but the thing was trying to convince an employer that someone who looked like he did could do the job. And acted like him. He wanted a job outside these walls, thinking it might save him from this continued craziness of solitary existence—a solitude that just had to kill him one day, he was sure—but he'd been like this so long it was difficult for anyone he met to picture him any other way. When he got back from that last interview he'd taken this long look at himself in the mirror and realized he hadn't a clue how he appeared to other people. He'd gone into that interview with dirt under his nails and white stuff at the corners of his mouth, and he hadn't even seen those things even though he'd made a studied self-examination before entering their building.

So they weren't about to give him a second look. They could not imagine anyone who looked like him working for them.

"It is a nice coat," he said. "I don't get many chances to wear it."

"Well, you should wear it more often," she replied. "Hey, maybe you could take me to the movies sometime. You could put that nice-looking jacket on and take me to the movies."

"I bet Tommy wouldn't be too happy with that." K.T. felt as if he had said something quite bold, but she didn't appear to react.

"Hey, you got a TV? Maybe there's a movie on now. You got your jacket and I got…" She held up her glass half full of juice. "Refreshments."

K.T. stood up, giddy with an odd sort of excitement. He hadn't felt so playful with a woman since before his older sister left home. She lived in Florida now, three kids, and they hadn't spoken in years. He went to the foot of the bed and started peeling away items from a pile of dirty clothes. "Ta da!" he said, revealing a dusty TV screen.

"Turn it on and come sit by me," she said, holding up her juice glass again. With a flourish K.T. slapped the "on" button, grabbed the sports jacket and slipped it on. It bunched at the shoulders, spoiling the gesture, and he had to pull and tug to make it feel right. Then he threw himself onto the bed beside her, thinking she would either run or laugh and in fact he didn't really care which, as long as she reacted to what he'd done in some way.

The TV came on in the middle of an old war picture. K.T. recognized some of the actors—he was pretty sure they were all dead. More and more this seemed to be the case for him: watching movies full of dead actors. What was worse, he suspected anyone younger than he wouldn't even know these actors were all dead—the notion would never cross their minds. The way they were in the movie would be the way these actors would be forever.

"I bet Silver Surfer would make a good movie-type hero," she said, close to his ear, almost whispering, slurring her words. "They should make a movie about him. Mr. No-face."

For just a brief moment he thought she was referring to him, that in his playful rush his face had slipped off and was now lost within the anxious clutter of the room. He pulled sweaty hands up to his mouth and nose and felt around, then jerked them away in embarrassment. "Oh, yeah." He laughed. "He'd make a great one all right."

She held the juice glass up to his lips. He was so close to her now he could see inside the eyeholes of her mask. Her eyes looked red, heavy and drugged. They would not fix on him. "Wait." She pulled the glass away. She took a small liquor bottle out of a big pocket in her dress, unscrewed it, and poured some into the juice. "Just to freshen it," she said, pressing it again to his lips. The glass was hard and cold and the liquor made his own eyes burn—she'd obviously been adding stuff from the bottle to the juice the whole time she'd been here. He closed his eyes and let her pour it into him. The edge of the glass bit like a hard cold kiss and then the warm fluid tongue inside his mouth and her hard swollen belly pressed up against him, nose filling with the perfume and the stench of her, and with his eyes closed he was seeing the both of them inside his monitor, trapped inside the tube, falling out of their clothes and then falling out of their faces until they were just this liquid descent of electrons down the screen and off the edge into nothing.

"Oh, sweet Jesus," he murmured into her neck as he moved up to kiss her, and feeling the fullness of her beneath him he couldn't help thinking of the sow with the frightened boy's head and the babies sucking and feeding and there's nothing the little boy can do to escape. "Jesus," he said again, more softly now as if to pray that terrible image out of his head, and wondered not for the first time if now and again he brushed against monsters.

She clung to him with a desperate strength that frightened him, and when he finally opened his eyes to tell her that they should be more careful about the baby, because he really was worried about the baby, frightened for her baby, he could see that her mask had slipped, more of her face was exposed, and the rows of circular cigarette burns like tiny ruined mouths all around both of her eyes.

"Tommy says I've got to wear my mask," she whispered huskily, and refitted it to her face, and tried to draw him back into her, into her smell and lips and eyes, into skin thin as desire, brief as a flash of phosphors on a smoked screen, but all he could think about was how was she ever going to market this, how was she going to sell this, how was she going to put the best face on this, and, at least for the moment, this was no longer a place he was prepared to go.

Hours later he could hear them across the courtyard of the mews arguing, and if there had been screams he would have gone over there and stopped them. He would have played the Silver Surfer in his mask that is no mask, and he would have stopped whatever was going on.

But there weren't any screams that night. Perhaps there had never been any screams.

Instead he stood and waited in his doorway, listening to the rhythmic rise and fall of their argument that might not be an argument, studying the tree that had never been a tree, admiring the way the cool halogen of the streetlights washed the rounded stones of cast concrete.

When he finally went back inside, he went first to the bathroom where he washed his face a very long time, then shaved away at the rough stubble of his beard until blood had welled in numerous nicks. The face that stared out at him was both terrible and new, one he had never seen before, and most likely would change to fit the given situation. It was the kind of face he had always wanted, it was the kind of face that might win him jobs and women, but he knew that at least for a few nights he would sleep with one eye open, a knife ready in hand for peeling the image away at the first sign of rebellion.

On his web site the self-portraits had apparently disappeared for good, broken and scattered into the ether. Just before dawn there was email, and an attachment: a picture of a fattened, battered cat with his face, so professionally done as to be seamless, so much of the cat in the line of his jaw and the tilt of his head, so much of his own terror as the feline head shifts to see the thing in fast pursuit.

THE COUGH

A tickle like the sound of a truck rumbling in the distance, felt in the chest, where bones join tissue and there are quantities of liquid for lubrication. Something was coming. Something was clearly out there. Something he didn't want to know about.

He'd had the cold for weeks. Three, four weeks. It didn't seem right, didn't seem natural. Weren't colds two week affairs? His wife had told him that at some time or other. He remembered the time last winter he'd been moaning and groaning, thinking he was going to die, angry because she wouldn't take care of him, wouldn't even sympathize, and she'd said, "Two weeks and it'll be gone. It's just a cold. Drink your orange juice."

Women had little sympathy for men. That had always been true. It was a way at getting back at their ill treatment under a patriarchy, he supposed. It was a man's world, and women had little sympathy. He really couldn't fault them for that, but it felt bad just the same.

Suddenly his body exploded into a fit of coughing. His face felt flushed. He could feel himself filling with fever. He could feel the tube of his throat constrict as he coughed, twisting at its root, trying to rip itself out of his body. Something was coming from a far distance. Something that didn't agree with him.

He spat something milky into the sink. His wife would have hated that. "Men have such disgusting habits," she used to say. He leaned over the sink and looked at what he had coughed up. Men did that, too—periodically they felt compelled to look at whatever came out of them. The globule in the sink was creamy, yet somewhat solid, like a small bit of half-digested flesh.

He wondered if what he was suffering from was akin to what they called "consumption" in the old days. He had no idea. But he was a man. Naturally he felt consumed. Men had a lot of things on their minds.

Suddenly the cough racked him again. His head jerked as if he'd been slapped. His wife had slapped him a couple of times, because of some dumb thing he'd said to her. He'd never hit her. He had no use for men who hit their wives.

But she should never have hit him.

Something was coming from a long distance away, something had come from a long distance, and now it was filling his throat. He thought that he would choke. He ran to the toilet bowl and coughed something up from his throat. It felt large and soft as if it were one of his internal organs as it passed his lips and plopped into the water.

He looked down. It was longish and pale, like an arm, and then it dissolved into the water.

Where was she, anyway? He couldn't remember. If it had been her making these noises of distress she would have expected him to come help her. But when he was the one who was sick, she hid herself. Marriage ought to be a two-way street.

At least she could have fed him something. He was hungry. He hadn't eaten anything all day, and he'd had way too much to drink last night in order to ease the pain in his throat and in other places he didn't like to talk about. He was hungry. Men had hungers. Where was she?

The next cough practically split him in two. It felt as if it had originated miles away. Something rushed through him, then past him as if on its way to an important destination. Where was she? He looked down at what he had brought forth from such a long distance away, and saw a soft, liquid, barely recognizable version of his wife's face floating in the bowl, a soft tinge of blood in the lips and cheeks. The image started to break up even as he impulsively jerked the lever to flush it all away.

And then he remembered.

YOU DREAMED IT

Cheryl woke up abruptly and rubbed her eyes as hard as she could. Her father had held her head over the toilet bowl; he was going to drown her. She was sure of it.

But then he had stopped all of a sudden, and she'd looked up into his faraway face. The face had been dark, and although she knew it was her father's face she really couldn't see it very well. Daddy? she'd said, but very softly. She wasn't even sure he could hear her. She wasn't even sure she wanted him to hear her.

He hadn't said anything. He picked her up, threw her over his shoulder, and carried her from the small bathroom to her bedroom at the end of the dark hallway. There was a bend in the hallway where the stairs came up. He was careful walking there; it would be easy to slip and drop her down the stairs.

Maybe he wanted to slip, she thought. But he didn't, this time. He'd hit her head real hard against the door frame when he walked into the hall; she'd sobbed once and held onto her cries, afraid he would get mad. Looking at the big staircase falling off into the dark helped her stop crying — it was so scary.

When they got to the end of the hallway he'd thrown her onto the bed. She made herself really stiff trying not to cry, but that made her back hurt when she hit the bed. She gasped once, then gasped again when he started pouring water on her. Glasses full of water, hitting her face harder and harder. Soaking into the bed. Soaking into her pajamas. Making everything wet, everything dripping with it. She finally began to cry; she couldn't help it. They would think she'd wet the bed again—Mommy and Daddy; she'd be in trouble.

He didn't say a thing. After he finished wetting her bed he turned and left.

Cheryl looked at her bed and reached out carefully with one hand. It was damp. So were her pajamas. She stared at the one window in the room, full of bright light, like water. She couldn't decide if she had dreamed or not.

Her father walked in. "Wet your bed again?" he said quietly.

Cheryl nodded her head and looked away.

"Well, that's all right. You know what you need to do now."

Cheryl got up and began stripping the bed. It was hard for her; the covers were tucked in real tight and all the blankets and the quilt were heavy, especially once they were wet, but she had to do it herself. That's what her daddy called "the deal."

He stepped out of her way as she waddled over to the hamper. She almost tripped at the last second, but then he grabbed her and set her upright. "Thank you," she said softly. He started to leave. "Daddy?" He turned around. "Did you take me to the bathroom last night?"

He crouched down then, and she saw his face: all pink and newly-shaven. He smiled with large thin lips and kissed her on the cheek. "No, sure didn't, Angel. You must have dreamed it."

She watched his face go away as he stood up. She nodded and he smiled again.

She got in trouble that day at school for staring out the window too much and not doing her work. She couldn't help it. Everything looked so blurry outside, like the sun had come down and made all the plants, cars, and buildings glow with a funny light. Or like she was seeing everything outside through water, but it wasn't raining. It was funny.

Later she looked into her lunch box and brought her marbles

out. They were red, blue, green, lots of different colors. Some you could even see through. A bunch of them had belonged to her first daddy, her real daddy, her mommy had told her. She liked looking at those the best. They looked so old. And they made her feel better. She brought them to school every day but she didn't play with them. She just liked to look. Somebody might steal them if she played.

Before dinner her daddy came home and stepped on her foot. Twice. He pretended he didn't notice and she pretended it didn't happen, even though it hurt a lot. But she pulled her feet up into the chair and sat on them, just to make sure he didn't do it again.

After dinner he passed by her in the upstairs hallway and nudged her into the wall. She hit her cheek and it cut a little.

A few minutes later he came out of his bedroom. She was sitting in the middle of the hall crying and holding her cheek. The blood felt hot and sticky on her fingers.

"Why, Cheryl! What happened?" he said and crouched down next to her, his wide face filling her vision.

"You... you pushed me!" she cried, sobbing, and for a moment was very afraid, afraid of what he would do to her now that she had said that. She shouldn't have said it, but she'd been hurt, and it made her forget.

"Why... how can you say that!" he said, looking really puzzled. Cheryl knew he was play-acting; his eyes were too wide and his mouth so large and open he looked like the giant chicken she liked so much on the cartoons. But she didn't like her daddy like this. She didn't like him at all.

"I'm... I'm sorry. I guess I fell." She looked down.

Then he was holding her, speaking softly to her, telling her that everything was going to be okay, and that he loved her very much. He talked to her just like she was his own real daughter. She hugged him back real hard, hoping maybe it was all true, though she really didn't think it was. Her old daddy had died so long ago she couldn't remember him, and when this new one came along last year and married her mother she used to dream sometimes that he was actually her real daddy come back to her, and that her mommy just didn't recognize him.

But that couldn't be true. Her real daddy wasn't like this one at all.

That night in bed she was thinking about her real daddy when the tall man with the dark face came in. She knew he was really her new daddy but now she was trying to think of him as a stranger, a bad dark stranger who pretended to help her by taking her to the bathroom so she wouldn't wet the bed but who was really an evil, bad man out to get her. It made her feel better that way. It made her feel safer when she had to be with her new daddy during the daytime.

The man with the dark face, the man with no face it was so dark, reached down and lifted her up out of the bed. "Time to use the bathroom," he said softly.

He took her down the hall into the bathroom and tried to crash her head against the doorframe. But she was too smart for him this time and put her hands over her head. She hurt her fingers when he bumped her into the doorframe but at least they didn't hurt as badly as her head had. Sometimes her head hurt so badly she couldn't sleep after that. And besides, her mommy asked funny questions about the bruises.

So she wasn't expecting it when he ran her face into the front of the sink. Her nose mashed and she couldn't breathe and it felt all funny. When she opened her mouth to cry he put his hand over her mouth and held it there so long she started feeling sleepy. Then he took it away. Then she was too sleepy to cry.

The next morning her mommy was all upset about her nose, wanting to know what happened.

"I can't remember," Cheryl said.

"But your nose is all bloody! Surely you know what happened?"

"Maybe Cheryl was playing where she shouldn't be playing and that's why she's afraid to tell us," her new daddy said, looking funny at her mommy.

Cheryl didn't say anything at first, then looked up at her mother. "I have bad dreams sometimes and they make things happen."

"Well, you didn't dream a bloody nose!" her mommy said.

"I... I think I must have tripped when Daddy was in my room last night."

Her new daddy looked at her mommy, then turned to Cheryl. "I wasn't in your room, Cheryl. You must have dreamed it."

Her mommy nodded her head slowly, and it looked to Cheryl like her mommy was very nervous. Cheryl nodded her head back. "I guess I did," she said.

"I know... you must have had a bad dream and fallen out of bed," her new daddy said.

Cheryl nodded silently, and the more she thought about it, the more she tried to think her new daddy was right. She wanted it to be true.

She sat for a long time on the stairs before bedtime listening to her mommy putting away the dishes, her new daddy talking to her in low sounds like a dog barking. For awhile it made her giggle, thinking that he sounded like a puppy, but then she got scared, and the staircase seemed darker than before.

"... getting to be a problem... her imagination..."

The words were suddenly easier to hear, and at first she couldn't understand why. But then she understood.

"She's delusional, Betty. All these dreams. And I think she's lying to you... to us, half the time..."

Her new daddy knew she was out on the stair listening. And he wanted to make sure she heard what he was telling her mommy.

"... something wrong with her, Betty. We love her. I love her. But we may have to send her away..."

Cheryl crawled up the steps carefully. She was afraid to stand up and walk, afraid she would make too much noise. And she didn't cry this time. It surprised her, but she didn't even feel like crying.

That night Cheryl woke up a little early. She looked at the

doorway, but there was no one there. The dark man with no face hadn't come yet.

She lay there thinking about what her daddy would do if he were in her place — her real daddy. Her good daddy.

She got up and went to her closet. She took out her bag of marbles. They were really old; she'd had them a long time. She took them and walked out the door.

She was really careful placing the marbles around the bend of the hallway, at the top of the stairs. She put them down one at a time, so that they made a nice pattern. The pattern looked a little like the moon. She put her real father's old marbles on the outside, and the newer marbles on the inside.

Then she got up to leave. There wasn't much light in the hallway. You couldn't even see the marbles on the dark carpet now.

She didn't have to wait long after she got back into bed. She heard her mommy and daddy's bedroom door opening, and the creakings and groanings of the hallway floor as the dark man with no face walked toward her bedroom.

Then there was the big crash, followed by a loud scream, and a lot of thumps and bangs as the dark man fell down the staircase.

"You must have dreamed it, Daddy," Cheryl said softly beneath the covers, giggling and snuggling closer to her pillows. "You dreamed it."

RAT CATCHER

Jimmy hadn't caught four hours sleep all week. Normally he was a dead man about five seconds after he hit the sheets. In fact he liked telling people "I work like a bastard for my sleepeye." Not that he didn't lie there staring at the ceiling a few hours now and then, but not like this, not for days, not for a week. Sometimes he might lie awake counting the tiles because he was trying to remember something, even though he might not know he was trying to remember something. Some special butt-saving part of his brain would nag at him until he'd think of that anniversary, birthday, or special favor for his boss that he'd completely forgotten. "Ah, Jimmy, thank you," he'd say when he remembered these things, flat on his back in bed. Sometimes Tess would nudge him with her elbow a little when this happened, pretending to be asleep but still letting him know he'd saved his butt by just a hair this time (she figured he'd forgotten something having to do with her and most of the time she was right).

But not this time. He didn't think his lack of sleep had anything to do with her. Not this time. What he forgot this time, he knew, came from somewhere deeper than that, from somewhere further back, off where the dog bled in the dark and the rats gathered round to lick the blood.

"Ah, Jimmy, thank you. . . ." he said, but quietly, not wanting Tess to hear. Off where the dog bled in the dark. . . .

Maybe he felt the scratching before he actually heard it. Later he'd wonder about that. He felt it up in his scalp, long and hard like fingernails scratching through a wooden door, the fingers bleeding from the effort and the mind spinning dizzy from the pain. Jimmy raised his head and looked toward the bedroom door—they always kept it open halfway and the hall light on because Miranda was just down the hall and at five years old she still hated the dark, almost as bad as Jimmy used to hate the dark. Almost as bad as he hated it now. They kept the door open because Jimmy wanted to be sure and hear her when she screamed, which she still did about once every two weeks. He didn't want to lose any time getting into his little girl's room.

Tess was always telling him that he coddled the kids. That was a funny word—he didn't think he'd ever heard anyone else use it besides his grandma, back when he was a kid. And maybe Tess was right. He'd never been able to talk much about what it is you do with kids—being a dad to them, disciplining them, that kind of thing—not the way Tess could. Sometimes she gave him these books to read, books on parenting by experts. He never got much out of them.

All Jimmy knew was to pay attention to them, love and protect them. And tell them when they did wrong, though after a while you couldn't stop them from doing wrong, just slow them down a little. Just doing that much wasn't easy, not like it sounded. The kids would find out soon enough that the world was worse than they'd ever imagined, and maybe they'd hate him a little at first because of that. But all he could do was try to keep them alive and teach them a few things that would help them keep themselves alive. And maybe someday they'd figure out he'd loved them and that he'd meant the best for them, even with all the mistakes he'd made. He figured love was mostly mistakes that turned out okay. And maybe he'd get lucky. Maybe he wouldn't be dead when that someday came around.

A small black dog, maybe a cat, came racing by the open

door, in and out of the little bit of light like a shadow pulled by a rubber band. On its way to Miranda's room, looked like. But they didn't own a dog, not since they put old Wooly to sleep. And their cat was white as a clean pillowcase.

Kids scream for all kinds of reasons. But even for the silly ones Jimmy had never been able to stand it. When Miranda's scream tore so raggedly out of the dark, he was up and heading out the door without even pulling down the covers. Tess made a little gasp of surprise behind him as the headboard rocked back and banged the wall. The whole house was shaking with his legs pounding down the hallway and Miranda screaming.

As soon as he reached his little girl's door he caught the sharp smell of pee, and when he slammed the light switch on he fully expected to find the rat up on the bed with her, marking her with his teeth and claws and marking the bed with his pee just to let Jimmy know whose was whose. But there was just Miranda huddled by herself, her face red as a beet (how do little kids make their faces go that color?), and the damp a gray flower opening up all around her tiny behind.

"Daddy! A big mousy! Big mousy!" she screamed, words he would have expected from her two years ago but not now (Dad! I'm a big girl now!), pointing a whole pudgy and shaking fist toward her open closet door. Jimmy ran back into the hallway and Miranda started screaming again; he could hear the baby squalling in the back room and Tess and Robert were out in the hall, Tess shouting What's wrong!, but Jimmy could hardly hear her over Miranda's Daddy!. He waved a hand at Tess trying to get her to stay back, jerked open the hall closet door and grabbed the heavy broom, and ran back into his daughter's room.

Where he slammed her closet door as far back as it would go and held the broom up, waiting.

Miranda's screams had choked off into hard, snotty breathing. He could feel Tess and Robert behind him at the door, Tess no doubt holding Robert's jaw in that way she had when she wanted him to know he shouldn't talk just now. Daddy's real busy.

Suddenly there was movement at the bottom of the closet: Miss Raggedy Ella fell over and Jimmy could see that half her face had been torn away into clouds of cotton and he just started waling away with the broom on Miss Ella and Barbie and Tiny Tears and Homer Hippo and the whole happy-go-lucky bunch until they were all dancing up and down and laughing with those big wide permanent grins painted on their faces (except for Miss Ella, who now had no mouth to speak of) and screaming just like Miranda did. "Daddy, stop! You're hurting them!"

"It's a rat! A rat, goddamit it!" He didn't know who he was yelling at; he just didn't know how they could be bothering him when there were rats in the house.

Eventually he stopped and when there wasn't any more movement he used the straw end of the broom to pull out Miranda's toys from the bottom of the closet one by one until it was empty.

He found a flap of loose wallpaper along the back wall above the yellowed baseboard. He lifted the flap up with the broom handle and discovered a four-inch hole in the plaster and lathe.

It took Miranda a long time to go back to sleep that night. She was trying to forget something but that part of her brain expert at saving your butt wasn't letting her forget so easily. Instead Jimmy knew that memory was getting filed back there where the rats lick the blood off the wounded dog.

Tess kept telling him, "It's all over now. Go to sleep, honey." And finally he pretended he had.

And thought about the rats he didn't want to think about living in his house, sniffing around his kids. He wasn't about to forget that one. He wasn't about to forget any of it.

He'd never thought that his momma had a dirty house, and he didn't think the other ladies in the neighborhood thought so either, else they wouldn't have kept coming over to the house, drinking coffee, eating little cakes his momma made and getting icing all over the Bicycle cards they played with. But this was Kentucky and it was pretty wet country up their valley down the ridge from the mines and half the rooms in that big old house they didn't use except for storage, and fully two-thirds of all those dressers his momma kept around were full of stuff—clothing, old letters, picture albums, bedding—and were never opened. His momma never threw away anything, especially if it came down from "the family," and she had taken charge of all of grandma's old stuff, who had never thrown away anything in her life either.

So it was that he found the nest of hairless little baby rats in that dresser drawer one day. He wasn't supposed to be messing with that dresser anyway. His momma would have switched him skinny if she'd have caught him in one of her dressers.

Back then they'd looked like nasty little miniature piglets to him, squirming and squealing for their momma's hairy rat-tit, but not quite real-looking, more like puppets, a dirty old man hiding inside the dresser making them squirm with transparent fishing line. He'd slammed the drawer shut right away and good thing, too, because if he hadn't then maybe that dirty old man would have reached his burnt arm out of the drawer and pulled him in. Jimmy's momma had never told him to be scared of rats but she sure as hell had told him all about the ragged, dirty old men who stayed down by the tracks and prowled the streets at night looking for young boys to steal.

He never told his momma about the rats either and they just seemed to grow right along with him, hiding in their secret places inside his momma's house. Like the rats he'd heard about up in the mines that grew big as beavers because they could hide there where nobody bothered them. He'd heard that sometimes the miners would even share their lunches with them. Then the summer he was twelve the rats seemed to be everywhere, in all the closets in the house and you could hear them in the ceilings and inside the floors running back and forth between the support beams under your feet and his momma got pretty much beside herself. He'd hear her crying in her bed at night sounding like his dear sweet little Miranda now.

He remembered feeling so bad because he was the man of the house, had been since he was a baby in fact and he knew he was supposed to do something about the rats but at twelve years old he didn't know what.

Then one day this big rat that should have been a raccoon or a beaver it was so big—a mine rat, he just knew it—came out from behind the refrigerator (that always felt so warm on the outside, smelling like hot insulation, perfect for a rat house) and ran around the kitchen while they were eating, its gray snake tail making all these S's and question marks on the marbled linoleum behind it. Jimmy's momma had screamed, "Do something!" and he had—he picked up the thick old broom and chased it, and that big hairy thing ran right up her leg and she screamed and peed all over herself and it dropped like she'd hit it and Jimmy broke the broom over it, but it started running again and he chased it down the cellar steps whacking it and whacking it with that broken piece of broom until the broom broke again over the rat's back and still it just kept going, now making its S's and question marks all over the dusty cellar floor so that it looked like a thousand snakes had been wrestling down there.

Jimmy kept thinking that this had to be the momma rat. In fact over the next year or so he'd prayed that what he had seen down there had been the momma, and not one of her children.

The rat suddenly went straight up the cellar wall and into a foot-high crawlspace that spread out under the living room floor.

"You get it, son?" His mother had called down from the kitchen door, her voice shaking like his grandma's used to.

He started to call back that he'd lost it, when he looked up at the crawlspace, then dragged an old chair over to the wall, and climbed up on the splintered seat for a better look.

Back in the darkness of the crawlspace there seemed to be a solider black, and a strong wet smell, and a hard scratch against the packed earth that shook all the way back out to the opening where his two hands gripped the wall.

The scratching deepened and ran and suddenly his face was

full of the sound of it as he fell back away from the wall with the damp and heavy black screeching and clawing at his face.

His momma called some people in and they got rid of the nests in the dressers and closets but they never did find the big dark momma he had chased into the cellar. At night he'd think about where that rat must have got to and he tried to forget what wasn't good to forget.

There was one more thing (isn't there always, he thought). They'd had a dog. Not back when he'd first seen the big momma rat, but later, because his momma had felt bad about what happened and he'd always wanted a dog, so she gave it to him. Jimmy named it Spot, which was pretty dumb but "Spot" had been a name that had represented all dogs for him since he was five or six, so he named his first dog Spot even though she was a solid-color, golden spaniel.

Just having Spot around made him feel better, although as far as he knew a dog couldn't help you much with a rat. Maybe she should have gotten him a cat instead, but he couldn't imagine a cat of any size dealing with that big momma rat.

Jimmy didn't think much about that dog anymore. Ah, Jimmy, thank you.

They had Spot four years. Jimmy was sixteen when the rats came back, a few at a time, and quite a bit smaller than the way he remembered them, but still there seemed to be a lot more of them each week and he'd dreamed enough about what was going to happen to him and his momma when there were enough of those rats.

Then he was down in the cellar one day when he saw this big shadow crawling around the side of the furnace and heard the scratching that was as nervous and deep as an abscess. He ran upstairs and got his dead daddy's shotgun that his momma had kept cleaned and oiled since the day his daddy died, and took it down to the dark, damp cellar, and waited awhile until the scratching came again, and then that crawling shadow came again, and then he just took aim, and fired.

When he went over to look at the body, already wondering

how he was going to dispose of that awful thing without upsetting his momma when she got home, he found his beautiful dog instead.

He'd started crying then, and shaking her, and ran back up the steps to get some towels (but why had she been crawling, and why hadn't she just trotted on over to him like she'd always done?), and when he got back down to the cellar with his arms full of every sheet and towel he could get his hands on, there had been all these rats gathered around the body of his dog, licking off the blood.

And now there were rats in his house, around his children.

The rat catcher, Homer Smith, was broad and rounded as an old Ford. Tess called Jimmy at work to tell him that the "rat man" had finally gotten there and Jimmy took the time off to go and meet him. When Jimmy first saw him, the rat catcher was butt-wedged under the front porch, his big black boots' soles out like balding tires, his baggy gray pants sliding off his slug-white ass as he pushed his way farther into the opening until all of a sudden Jimmy was thinking of this huge, half-naked fellow crawling around under their house chasing rats. And he was trying not to giggle about that picture in his head when suddenly the rat catcher backed out and lifted himself and pulled his pants up all in one motion too quick to believe. Homer Smith was big and meaty and red-faced like he'd been shouting all morning, and looking into his face Jimmy knew there was nothing comical about this man at all.

"You got rats," Homer Smith said, like it wasn't true until he'd said it. Jimmy nodded, watching the rat catcher's lips pull back into a grin that split open the lower half of his bumpy brown face. But the high fatty cheeks were as smooth and unmoved as before, the eyes circled in white as if the man had spent so much time squinting that very little sun ever got to those areas. The eyes inside the circles were fixed black marbles with burning highlights. "Some call me out to look at their rats and it comes up nothing but little mousies they coulda chased away their own selves with a lighter and a can of hairspray. If they had a little hair on their chests that is." Miranda's "mousies" sounded lewd and obscene coming from Smith's greasy red lips. "But rats now, they don't burn out so good. That hair of theirs stinks to high heaven while it's burning, but your good size mean-ass rat, he don't mind burning so much. And you, son…" He raised his fist. "You got rats."

Jimmy stared at the things wriggling in the rat catcher's fist: blind, pale and constantly moving, six, maybe eight little hairless globs of flesh, all alike, all as blank and featureless as the rat catcher's fingers and thumb, which now wriggled with the rat babies like their own long-lost brothers and sisters. "How many?" Jimmy asked, glancing down at his feet.

"How many what?" Smith asked, gazing at his fistful of slick wriggle. He reached over with a finger from the other hand and flicked one of the soft bellies. It had a wet, fruity sound. Jimmy could see a crease in the rat skin from the hard edge of the nail. A high-pitched squeak escaped the tiny mouth.

Jimmy turned away, not wanting to puke on his new shoes. "How many rats? How many days to do the job? Any of that," he said weakly.

The rat catcher grinned again and tossed the babies to the ground where they made a sound like dishrags slapping linoleum. "Oh, you got lots, mister. Lots of rats and lots and lots of days for doing this job. You'll be seeing lots of me the next few weeks."

And of course the rat catcher hadn't lied. He arrived each morning about the time Jimmy was leaving for work, heavy gauge cages and huge wood and steel traps slung across his back and dangling from his fingers. "Poison don't do much good with these kind o' rats," Smith told him. "They eat it like candy and shit it right out again. 'Bout all it does is turn their assholes blue." Jimmy wasn't about to ask the rat catcher how he'd come by the information.

If he planned it right Jimmy would get home each afternoon

just as Smith was loading the last sack or barrel marked "waste" up on his pickup. The idea that there were barrels of rats in his house was something Jimmy tried not to think about.

If he planned it wrong, however, which happened a lot more often than he liked, he'd get there just as the rat catcher was filling the sacks and barrels with all the pale dead babies and greasy-haired adults he'd been piling up at one corner of the house all day. Babies were separated from the shredded rags and papers they'd been nested in, then tossed into the sacks by the handfuls, so many of them that after a while Jimmy couldn't see them as dead animals anymore, or even as meat, more like vegetables, like bags full of radishes or spring potatoes. The adults Smith dropped into the barrels one at a time, swinging them a little by their slick pink tails and slinging them in. When the barrels were mostly empty, the sound the rats made when they hit was like mushy softballs. But as the barrels filled the rats made hardly a sound at all on that final dive: no more than a soft pat on a baby's behind, or a sloppy kiss on the cheek.

Jimmy had figured Smith was bound to be done after a few days. But the man became like a piece of household equipment, always there, always moving, losing his name as they started calling him by Tess's name for him, "the rat man," as if he looked like what he was after, when they were able to mention him at all. Because sometimes he made them too jumpy even to talk about, and the both of them would stay up nights thinking about him, even though they'd each pretend to the other that they were asleep. A week later he was still hauling the rats out of there. It seemed impossible. Jimmy started having dreams about a mine tunnel opening up under their basement, and huge, crazy-eyed mine rats pouring out.

"I don't like having that man around my kids," Tess said one day.

Jimmy looked up from his workbench, grabbing onto the edge of it to keep his hands from shaking. "What's he done?"

"He hasn't done anything, exactly. It's just the way he looks, the way he moves."

Jimmy thought about the rats down in their basement, the rats in their walls. “He’s doing a job, honey. When he’s done with the job he’ll get out of here and we won’t be seeing him anymore.”

“He gives me the creeps. There’s something, I don’t know, a little strange about him.”

Jimmy thought the rat man was a lot strange, actually, but he’d been trying not to think too much about that. “Tell you what, I’ve got some things I can do at home tomorrow. I’ll just stick around all day, see if he’s up to anything.”

Jimmy spent the next day doing paperwork at the dining room table. Every once in a great while he’d see the rat man going out to his truck with a load of vermin, then coming back all slick smiles and head nodding at the window. Then Jimmy would hear him in the basement, so loud sometimes it was like the rat man was squeezing himself up inside the wall cavities and beating on them with a hammer.

But once or twice he saw the rat man lingering by one of the kid’s windows, and once he was scratching at the baby’s screen making meow sounds like some great big cat, a scary, satisfied-looking expression on his face. Then the rat man looked like the derelicts his momma had always warned him about, the ones that had a “thing” for children. But still Jimmy wasn’t sure they should do anything about the rat man. Not with the kind of rat problem they had.

When he talked to her about it that night Tess didn’t agree. “He’s weird, Jimmy. But it’s more than that. It’s the way the kids act when he’s around.”

“And how’s that?”

“They’re scared to death of him. Miranda sticks herself off in a corner somewhere with her dolls. Robert gets whiny and unhappy with everything, and you know that’s not like him. He just moves from one room to the next all day and he doesn’t seem to like any of his toys or anything he’s doing. But the baby, she’s the worst.”

Jimmy started to laugh but caught himself in time, hoping

Tess hadn't seen the beginnings of a smile on his lips. Not that this was funny. Far from it. But this idea of how the baby was reacting to the rat man? They called their youngest child "the baby" instead of by her name, because she didn't feel like a Susan yet. She didn't feel like anything yet, really—she seemed to have no more personality than the baby rats the rat man had thrown down outside the house. Tess would have called him disgusting, saying that about his own daughter, but he knew she felt pretty much the same way. Some babies were born personalities; Susan just wasn't one of those. This was one of those things that made mommies and daddies old before their time: waiting to see if the baby was going to grow into a person, waiting to see if the baby was going to turn out having much of a brain at all.

So the idea of "the baby" feeling anything at all about the rat man made no sense to Jimmy. He felt a little relieved, in fact, that maybe they'd made too much out of this thing. Maybe they'd let their imaginations get away from them. Then he realized that Tess was staring at him suspiciously. "The baby?" he finally said. "What's wrong with the baby?"

"Susan," Tess replied, as if she'd been reading his mind. "Susan is too quiet. Like she's being careful. You know the way a dog or a cat stops sometimes and gets real still because it senses something dangerous nearby? That's Susan. She's hardly even crying anymore. And you try to make her laugh—dance that teddy bear with the bright blue bib in front of her, or shake her rattle by her face—and she doesn't make a sound. Like she knows the rat man's nearby and she doesn't want to make a noise 'cause then he'll figure out where she is."

In his head Jimmy saw the rat man prowling through the dark house, his baby holding her breath, her eyes moving restlessly over the bedroom shadows. "Maybe he'll be done soon."

"Christ, Jimmy, I want him out of here! And I know you do, too!"

"What reason could I give him? We're just talking about 'feelings' here. We don't really know anything."

"What reasons do we need? We hired the man—we can fire him just as easy."

"Easy?"

"You're scared of him, Jimmy! I've never seen you so scared. But these are our kids we're talking about!"

"He makes me a little nervous, I admit," he said. "What you said about Susan makes me nervous as hell. And I am thinking about the kids right now, and how I can keep things safe for them around here."

"So we just let him stay? We just let him sneak around our kids doing god-knows-what?"

"We don't know he's doing anything except acting a little eccentric. We could fire him and the police could force him off our property, but that doesn't help us any with what might happen later."

"Later," she repeated. Jimmy couldn't bear how scared she looked. "What are we going to do?"

"I'm staying home again tomorrow. I'll park the car down the steet and hide in the house. If he's doing anything he shouldn't, he probably figures he can avoid your one pair of eyes. But tomorrow you'll be following your normal schedule and I'll be your extra pair of eyes. Between the two of us we shouldn't miss much." Jimmy looked down at the floor, thinking of the beams and pipes and electrical conduit hidden there. He listened for the rats, but the only scratches he heard were the ones inside his head.

The rat man came out exactly at nine in the A. M. like always. You could set your clock by him. He started unloading all his equipment, including the sacks and the metal barrel he threw the adult rats in. Jimmy crouched low by the master bedroom window, watching for anything and everything the rat man did. The first sign of weirdness, he thought, and he'd be hauling his kids' asses out of there. Tess went to work in the kitchen; they agreed it'd be best to pretend she was having a normal day.

The rat man disappeared around the corner of the house

with the big metal barrel. Jimmy was thinking about shifting to another room when he came back, holding four stiff rats by the tails, their black coats grayed with dust. No way he could've caught and killed them that quick, he thought. The rats appeared to have been dead a good day at least. Jimmy watched as the rat man waddled up to the corner where the house turned into an "L," the corner with the window to the baby's room. He watched as the rat man dangled the stiff rats against the rusting screen, clucking and cooing, rubbing his fingers up and down the smooth, hairless tails, talking to Jimmy's baby through the screen and smiling like he didn't realize where he was, like he was off in another place entirely.

Off where dogs bleed in the dark and the rats gather round to lick the blood.

All day long Jimmy watched as the rat man sneaked dead adult rats and hairless baby rats out of his rusted green pickup and planted them in the crawl spaces under the house only to haul them out again and replace them in the barrel and the sacks. The same ones, over and over. Jimmy wondered how many rats they'd actually had in the first place. A dozen? Six? Four? Just the one, trapped back under Miranda's bedroom, and coming into the rat man's hand easier than a hungry kitten?

Now and then the rat man would come out with something wrapped in a towel or a rag, cradling it carefully in his arms like it was his own baby. Jimmy couldn't quite credit the gentleness he was seeing in the rat man; he looked silly, really. Jimmy wondered why the rat man would want some of the rats bundled up.

Right after the rat man left for the day Jimmy told the whole story to Tess. "I wasn't about to confront him on it here," he said.

"Well, if he's just a con artist then we can call the police."

"He's a helluva lot more than that—I think we've both figured that one. That little office he has in town is closed and there's no home phone number listed. So I'm going to have to go out to his place tonight. I'm going to tell him not to come around here anymore."

"What if he says no?"

"He's not allowed to say no, honey. I'm not going to let him."

"What if I say no, Jimmy?" Her voice shook.

"I don't think you're going to say no. I think you're going to be thinking about the kids, and that crazy man dangling rats in front of their faces like they were baby toys." He stroked her shoulder. After a few seconds she looked away. And Jimmy grabbed his coat and went out to the car.

The rat man lived out past the empty industrial parks on the north end of the city. Here the municipal services weren't so good, the streets full of ragged holes like they'd just run short of asphalt, the signs faded, with a permanent, pasted-on look to the trash layering the ditch lines.

It wasn't hard finding the right house. "The rat catcher man? He lives down the end of that street don't-cha-know." The old man was eager to tell him even more information about the rat man, but these were stories Jimmy didn't want to hear.

The rat man's house didn't look much different from any other house in that neighborhood. It was a smallish box, covered with that aluminum siding you're supposed to be able to wash off with a hose. A small porch contained a broken porch swing. There were green curtains in the window. A brown Christmas wreath hung on the front door even though it was April. Two trash cans at the curb overflowed with paper and rotten food. And the foot-high brown grass moved back and forth like a nervous shag carpet.

What was different about the rat man's yard was all the tires that had been piled there, stacked into wobbly-looking towers eight or nine feet tall, bunches of them sitting upright like a giant black snake run through a slicer, tangled together in some parts of the yard like a slinky run through the washer. Some of the tires were full of dirt and had weeds growing out of them. Some of the tires looked warped and burnt like they'd had to be scraped off somebody's car after some fiery journey.

But it was the nervous grass that kept pulling at Jimmy's gaze. It wiggled and shook like the ground underneath it was getting ready to turn somersaults.

When Jimmy moved through it on the way to the rat man's door, it scratched at the sides of his boots. When Jimmy climbed the porch steps it slicked long, trembling fingers up around his ankles, making slow S-curves and question marks that set him shivering almost—it was crazy—with delight.

When Jimmy actually got to the door he could hear the layers of scratch and whisper building behind him, but he didn't turn around. The scratching got louder and Jimmy found himself angry. He started to knock on the rat man's door but once he got his hand curled into a fist he just held it there, looked at it and made the fist so tight the fingers went white. The scratching was in his ears and in his scalp now, and suddenly he was in a rage at the rat man and couldn't get that picture out of his head: the rat man dangling those dead monster babies in front of Jimmy's baby's window.

He held back his fist before he punched through the rotting door and instead moved to the dingy yellow window at the back of the rat man's porch. He let go of the fist and used the open hand to shield his eyes from the late afternoon glare when he pressed his face against the glass.

He saw the rat man's back bobbing up and down like a greasy old sack moving restlessly with its full complement of dying rat babies. The walls of the room were lined with a hodge-podge of shelving: gray planks and old wooden doors cut into strips and other salvage rigged in rows and the shelves full of glass jars like his grandmother's root cellar packed with a season's worth of canning.

Jimmy couldn't tell what was in those jars. It looked like yellow onions, potatoes maybe.

The rat man was taking something out of a sack. He moved, and Jimmy could see a small table, and little bundles of rags on it. The rat man picked up the bundles gently and filled his arms with them. Then he headed toward a dark brown, greasy-looking door at the back of the room.

Jimmy stepped off the porch and moved toward the side of the house. The rat man's grass seemed to move with him, pushing against his shoes and rippling as he passed. He looked down and now and then saw a gray or black hump rise briefly over the grass tops before sinking down inside again.

The first window on that side was dark and even with his face pushed up into the dirty screen he could see nothing. A tall dresser or something had been pushed up against the window on the other side.

The second window glowed with a dim yellow light. Jimmy moved toward it, through grass alive with clumps and masses that rubbed against his boots, crawled over his ankles, and scratched at his pant legs.

A heavy curtain had been pulled across the window, but it gapped enough in the middle to give Jimmy a peep-hole. Inside, the rat man was unwrapping the bundles. Around the room were more shelves, but here they had been filled with children's toys: dolls, teddy bears, stuffed monkeys and rabbits, tops and cars and jack-in-the-boxes and every kind of wind-up or pull-toy Jimmy had ever seen. Some of them looked shiny brand-new as if they'd just come out of the box. Others looked as old as Jimmy and older, the painted wood or metal dark brown or gray with layers of oily-looking dust.

The rat man put his new toys up on the shelf: a Miss Raggedy Ella doll, Tiny Tears, Homer Hippo, GI Joe, a plastic Sherman tank, a baby rattle, and a teddy bear with a bright blue bib. Toys that belonged to Jimmy's kids. And then the rat man picked up the last, slightly larger bundle, and placed it in a pink bassinet in the middle of the room, where he unwrapped it and rearranged the faded blankets.

Suddenly Jimmy felt the rats clawing at his ankles, crawling up his legs.

He turned so quickly—thinking he'd run to the porch and

break through the door—that he stumbled and fell on his knees. Instantly he had rats crawling up on his back, raking at his legs, several hanging by their claws and teeth from the loose front of his shirt. He stood and brushed them off him, finally grabbing one that just wouldn't let go with his hands around its belly and squeezing until it screamed and dropped.

All around him the towered and twisting mass of tires was alive with dark rats, scrambling over each other as they climbed and tumbled through the insides and over the outsides of the black casings. He didn't make it to the porch without losing a few hunks of skin here and there. The rats gathered round to lick the blood. . . .

The rat man's door disintegrated the second time Jimmy plowed into it with his shoulder, but not without a couple of hard splinters lodging painfully into the top of his arm. He stumbled into the front room and crashed into the far wall where the shelves of old wood began pulling away from the wall, dumping row after row of Mason jars onto the floor.

His feet slid on the spilled gunk. He could feel soft lumps smashing under the soles of his shoes. He staggered and grabbed the edge of a shelf, bringing down more of the jars. He started moving toward the greasy brown door at the back of the room as if in slow-motion, looking down at his shoes and moving carefully so that he wouldn't slash himself on the broken glass, but all the time screaming, yelling at himself to get his ass in gear and get to that bedroom at the back of the rat man's house.

He saw, but didn't think about, the bodies of the hundreds of hairless little rat babies bursting open under his shoes and smearing across every inch of the wooden floor.

He felt himself sliding, beginning to fall, as he jerked the door open and headed down a pitch black hallway toward a dim yellow rectangle of light at the other end. He pushed at the invisible walls of the hallway to keep himself upright and raced toward that rectangle, the walls going away around him as in a dream.

He wasn't aware of pushing open the door to the back room. It just seemed to dissolve at the touch of his hands.

Homer Smith, the rat man, was bent over the pink bassinet, cooing and making little wet laughing sounds. Later Jimmy would wonder why it was the rat man hadn't paid any attention to the ruckus in the front part of his house.

Homer looked up, his hands still inside the bassinet, as Jimmy hit him across the face as hard as he could. He fell to his knees with a noise like thunder, then looked up at Jimmy, then looked around at all his toys, smiled a little, like he wanted Jimmy to play with him. Off where the dog bled in the dark.... Jimmy kicked him in the ribs this time, with boots still smeared and sticky.

Homer doubled over without a sound, then he looked up at Jimmy again, and his face was as soft and unfocused as a baby's.

Jimmy thought about his baby in the bassinet, but couldn't quite bring himself to look yet. He glanced around the room instead and saw the broom propped in one corner. He stepped over to it, still aware that Homer wasn't moving, picked it up and brought it down across Homer's left cheekbone. The straw-end snapped off like a dry, dusty flower head and Jimmy used the broken handle to whip Homer's face until it was a bloody, frothy pudding, Homer's head snapping back and forth with each blow but still Homer stayed upright, leaning forward on his knees. Jimmy couldn't believe it, and it scared him something terrible.

He kept thinking about the baby, but couldn't keep his eyes off the baby catcher, the baby snatcher. Finally he took the ragged, broken end of the broom handle and held it a couple of feet from Homer's throat. Jimmy could feel the weight of the pink bassinet behind him, and the thing wrapped up inside it, not moving, not crying, keeping still as if watching to see what would happen, but Jimmy knew it wasn't just keeping still. It was dead. Susan was dead. He hadn't checked on her before he came out here after the rat man and he should have known, watching the rat man carrying all those swaddled objects out of his house like that. He should have known.

At last Homer Smith raised his bloody head and stared at the sharp stick Jimmy had poised at his throat and seeing what Jimmy was ready to do Homer began to cry a wet, blood-filled cry, like a baby, just like a baby Jimmy thought, and it reminded him of lots of things, not all of it bad, as he drove the sharp end of that stick as hard as he could into the soft skin of Homer's throat.

The dying took a few minutes, Homer trying to pull the stick out but not being able to. Jimmy threw up over by the bassinet until he had nothing left to heave. Finally he got to his feet again and stood over his baby, hesitated, then slowly unwrapped the blanket from around her.

And found two dead black rats there, curled around each other like Siamese twins. Homer had dressed each in baby doll clothes.

Jimmy felt the scratching up in his scalp, long and hard like fingernails clawing through a wooden door, long before he actually heard it. And then the sound of hundreds of pale tongues, lapping.

He turned and looked off where the dog bled in the dark at Homer Smith's body, and the hundreds of rats gathered round to lick the blood.

BLOOD KNOT

"Just a damn knot. You can't untie it; you can't burn it off. Older you get the tighter it gets. Might as well accept it, 'cause that's the way it is. What else you going to do? Kill everybody in the family? Jesus Christ, it's a goddamned blood knot."

I heard my daddy say this when I was thirteen, fourteen, something like that. We were at our last family reunion: daddy, me and sis, and daddy's fourth wife, June. "Junebug," he called her—I guess because she was so much younger than him.

Flashforward ten years later and there daddy is in a hospital bed coughing his lungs out. He pulls me closer—I was in my army fatigues—and with breath that smelled like shit he tells me, "I married my June bug 'cause she was so young I knew the rest of the family wouldn't approve and they'd have nothing to do with her. Had me a ready-made excuse to stay away from the rest of them, give myself some breathin' room. With your family, well, you're who you are but then you're not who you are, you know what I mean? Because you can't move. You can't change. Too bad she was so damn dumb."

I thought he was a fool. He had everything I'd ever wanted: kids, and a house, and more than one wife who'd loved him more than he'd deserved, surely more than was good for her. By then I'd found out that I had no talent for girlfriends, not even bad ones. They never lasted long enough to get bad. They never lasted long enough to be a pleasant memory after they were over. I was too reckless, or I wasn't reckless enough. I was too kind, or I wasn't kind enough. Something. Whatever it was that brought out the skittishness, the scared dog look, in those women, I had. In plentiful supply. I asked, even begged sometimes, for answers, and it was always something like, "maybe it's the way you talk," or "maybe it's all that stuff you think about." And that was if I really made them give me an answer. But they didn't know. I didn't know, and they didn't know. Hell, I thought being a little weird attracted some women. But not in my case.

"Some things are fated. Maybe you've got bad fate, or something, Harold." That was Linda, the night before she left me. She held me, and she let me cry in her bed, and she listened while I spilled my guts about needing a family of my own, someone I could love like I was supposed to, and she was good, so good she brushed away my embarrassment when she brushed away my tears, and the next day she left me. Fate, I guess.

Well, fuck her. She was good to me that night, but fuck her.

I'm not sure, but I think Daddy killed June one night, shortly after I'd turned eighteen. I don't know—we just never saw her around again. There'd been a lot of noise, a lot of drinking. I'm sorry to say that at the time I felt a big load had been taken off, because of the way she looked at me, the funny way she made me feel. Daddy always said she never really was part of the family. She kept herself apart and, after all, she wasn't blood. And she was young, too young to understand him, or us, or much of anything about living I guess. Maybe that was why I could feel about her the way I did—my own stepmother after all. She wasn't blood, and like he'd always told me himself, blood is everything.

I don't know what Daddy would have made of my three daughters. I don't want to know. If he had lived I wouldn't have let him anywhere near them—even if somebody'd pulled off his arms and snipped off his balls. I had that dream once, where somebody cut him up like that. He didn't even scream. In fact he thanked the man, the man in the shadows holding the razor. He smiled and said "Thank you very much—I sure needed that," even as the blood spurted from his crotch like some kind of orgasm that had been going on too long. I don't know if it was a nightmare or not.

"It don't matter if you like your family or not. You're tied to 'em; might as well accept that. It's in the blood."

So yeah, it finally happened. I met my own June, only her name was Julie, and she was quite a bit younger, and not very smart. I oughta be embarrassed saying that I guess. But I'm not. I did love her, still do, I'm sure. A person doesn't have to be smart, or the right age, for you to love them.

I'm never going to know I guess if she really loved me, or if it was just because she was younger, and not knowing what love is really, and then the girls came along, and so like any good mother—and I'll always swear that she was a good mother—she stuck with the father of those children, however strange his thinking, and said that she loved him with all of her heart. And maybe she did. Maybe she did. I've never really understood women. Not my wife. And not my daughters.

But oh, I've loved my daughters. All three of them, precious as tears. Only a couple of years apart—Julie for some crazy reason thought I wanted a son so she insisted we keep trying, but I was overjoyed, I felt blessed, to have daughters—but my oldest Marcie was small for her age, and my youngest Ann was taller than average, and middle daughter Billie was just like the middle bear, just right, so the three of them together were taken all the time for triplets. We were always told how adorable they were, how beautiful. People were just naturally attracted to them. And the boys? Boys are always just naturally drawn to something a little different. I know.

Things were pretty much okay until the girls got to be teenagers. Don't tell me about that being a hard time of life, I know that's a hard time of life but knowing that still doesn't help a father much. The girls started wanting dates and it was okay with their mother because Julie just didn't know no better I guess. They were too damned young and I said so but of course they went and done it anyway and after awhile I just got tired of watching them and chasing after them and let them just go right ahead and date too young and ruin their lives—what was I supposed to do?

Oh, I still loved them you can count on that but I have to say I was mad at them most of the time.

But my girls sure looked beautiful in those date dresses of theirs—so beautiful I couldn't stand to look at them when they were all dolled up.

They tell you on Oprah and Donahue and every other damn program what to do with your kids but they don't tell you a damn thing that helps. They act like kids and their families are separate people that have to negotiate every damn thing. They just don't understand it that a family's got to be all tied up in knots you can't get loose of no matter how hard you try. Cut those knots apart and somebody's bound to wind up bleeding to death on the floor.

I don't know if my girls knew I still loved them. I couldn't be sure cause I stopped telling them I loved them once the oldest got to be thirteen. That might not have been the right thing to do but I just didn't feel right, telling a young fresh-faced beauty of thirteen that I loved her. Perverts do that, not a good family man. Not a father.

Besides they shoulda known. They shoulda always known. We were blood weren't we, all tied together?

The girls all started their periods early. Hell, the youngest—my baby Ann—was nine, and you know that can't be right. My wife handled all that stuff of course but she still talked to me about it—I don't know why women like to talk about such things. She told me the baby was young to be having her period but that was becoming more and more common these days, but as far as I was concerned that was hardly any kind of recommendation. Not much right about these days what with baby girls having periods and watching actual live sex acts on the TV when their daddies ain't around. And their mothers making it a secret, too. Mothers and daughters, they always have these secrets that no man alive can understand.

What was I supposed to do about any of it? What could I do?

People expect the man to change the world but the world is a damned hard thing to change—it just rolls on pretty much the way it wants to until it runs right over you.

Sometimes all the females in the house had their periods at the same time and the blood stank up everything and I'd wake up in the middle of the night and sometimes Julie wouldn't be in the bed and then she'd come back and say why she'd just been down the hall in the bathroom but the bathroom was near where the girls slept and I'd think every time, I'd sit there in the dark and think, what if Julie and my girls are down the hall drinking some man's blood?

Now, I know that ain't true and it's a pretty crazy way to think but I wasn't always sure at the time. My girls' breasts were getting bigger every day and it seemed to me they weren't eating enough at meals to be puttin' on that kind of weight.

Then one day I thought I had it figured out—they were bleeding out and they were getting breasts and hair in return, breasts and hair so they could fuck as many guys as they could before they got too old to enjoy it.

And of course what they were bleeding out was the family blood, dumping it like it was something dirty and all used up and something they didn't need anymore.

They were fools, of course. Like you could untie the knot by disrespecting it that way. What right did they have anyway? I was tied to them so hard I wasn't ever going to get loose so why should they get their freedom? What had they ever done to earn it? Here I was having done everything for Julie and the girls and I was going to be tied to it forever. I wasn't ever going to be rid of the taste of their blood, their dirt, their flesh. I was going to die choking on it.

I can't even say I didn't like the taste of that knot. That salty, ocean taste like it was everything we'd ever come from for thousands of years. I can't say I didn't like it—maybe you have something shoved in your face long enough you hate it for awhile but maybe there comes a point—years maybe—where it's been shoved there so often you just start liking it again. You feed on it and after awhile maybe that's all you live for practically.

That was me and my wife and my girls. Our blood knot. I loved them and I hated them and then I loved them so much I couldn't be without them, couldn't let them out of my sight. It was like I had the taste of them in my mouth all the time and I was liking that taste more and more, and I just couldn't live without it, no way.

If they'd stayed home more often things probably would've turned out okay. Maybe I would get tired of them, tired of the taste and smell of them, and I'd get tired of it all like I did when they first wanted to date and then I'd just let them do what they damn well pleased. Julie could have made them stay home if she'd had the mind, but I married her too young and she was just too damned dumb. A good mother in every other way but too dumb for my girls I'm sorry to say.

I loved my girls, I loved them dear. I started trying to tell them that so maybe they'd stay at home but it didn't work.

My youngest, my baby Ann, she even laughed at me and what's a man supposed to do with that? I would've hit her real hard right then and there but at that point I still couldn't hit my baby girl. The other two, but not her.

I should've had boys, should've made Julie give me boys but I never could've loved boys that way. I don't know if that's a good thing, or a bad thing.

Let me explain something: I know I wasn't always the best father and husband. If I had been I wouldn't have let things get so far. A good father and husband keeps a lid on things, keeps things from going so far. Keeping things from going so far—with his kids, his wife, with the neighbors—that's the main thing a father's supposed to be doing. And I know I failed at that one.

Things collect, and they don't go away. Things get together, you get too many of them, and then things go too far.

Knots get untied. Blood gets spilled on the old, dry wooden floors and the floor soaks it up so fast you can't believe it, lots faster than you can clean it up and pretty soon the whole floor is stained red and everything you look at looks red.

I think they all four must have been having their period. They weren't complaining about it but the whole house smelled like it and I tasted it in every meal for two days and I breathed that blood in every time I opened my mouth and all my clothes smelled like it and even the newspaper and two nights running my dreams were so red I couldn't make out a thing in them.

Marcie had come back from one of her "dates." Fuck fests more like it but a father can't say that in front of his daughters and still be a good father. I just smiled at her and asked, "Have a nice time?" And she just stared at me looking scared. There was no point in that—I loved her—didn't she know that?

Then I saw that my baby Ann was with her.

"What the fuck!" I yelled and immediately felt bad, saying the F word in front of my girls but it was already out there and I couldn't get it back inside.

"Had me my first date, Daddy!" Ann piped up with her little dollie's voice. "Mom said it was okay with her. Me and Marcie, we doubled."

I couldn't say a damn thing, just stared at the two of them all made up like models, or whores. They'd put me down in a box, and I couldn't see a way to climb my way out. I turned around and went into the bedroom and closed the door, sat down to think. Once you got a family, you don't get too much time to think.

I felt all loose with myself. I felt untied. The women in a family, they have a way of doing that to their men.

Being in a family is like being in a dream. You don't know if it's a good dream, or a bad dream. You don't know if you're up or down. Everything moves sideways, until before you know it you're back where you started again, like you hadn't moved anywhere at all. That's where I was, moving sideways so fast but not going nowhere.

My girls, they started the untying. It wasn't me that did that part. My beautiful, beautiful girls. I just finished what they started.

But when you start untying that blood knot, it's more blood than anyone could imagine. It goes back forever, that blood. You taste it and you breathe it and it stains the floor and it stains the walls and it stains the skin until you're some kind of cartoon running around stabbing and chopping and tasting.

My babies' breasts like apples, like sweet onions, like tomatoes.

Once they were all in the blood it was like they were being born again, crying out "I love you daddy," and I could kiss them and there was not a damn thing wrong with any of it, cause daddies are supposed to love their babies.

Because they're your blood, you see. And you're tied to them forever.

THE CARVING

She'd told her friends how they'd met, how after a week's courtship they'd married.

True in part but there'd been no courtship. She'd fallen for this man, for the strength and sureness of his hands, and she'd asked him to marry her. And because he was the man he was, needing an ordered place where art might happen, he'd said yes. Two years later the baby was born, and she'd set out to make this strange artist love his only child.

Out on the deck his exacting hands sent into wood chisels as sharp as dread. Flakes rose into bright air and fluttered the long descent to the rocks below. He did not mark the wood, did not reduce it with machinery before his preliminary cuts. Outlines, he said, were no use for freeing the true shapes within.

Their boy always played near his father's working, even when the man's careless indifference brought him pain. For the boy knew that the carver could not keep his hands off the thing he had made, the thing he had freed from unfeeling matter, and in this way the boy got his hugs and impromptu dances and a quick toss in the air that made him believe in wings.

A steady thok as steel parted wood a hundred years old. She imagined their son sitting patiently, watching those steady hands, waiting for his toss.

Her friends said he was too self-absorbed, that life with such a man would leave her empty and desperate for talk. But she knew what her son knew: there could be no greater love than that which the artist bore for the thing he had freed from the world.

Such unshakable focus, she thought, opening the door that led out onto the deck and her husband's working. The steady rhythm of hammer and hand uplifted her in just the hearing, so that she, too, felt winged and freed from a mundane world. She looked for her son, expecting him there waiting for his little toss, but her son was not there.

Her husband sat hunched over his work. For a moment she was furious about his lack of care. Where was their son? Then following the flight of chips, white and red and trailing, over the railing's edge and down onto the rocks, she saw the fallen form, the exquisite work so carelessly tossed aside, the delicate shape spread and broken, their son.

She turned to the master carver, her mouth working at an uncontrolled sentence. And saw him with the hammer, the bloody chisel, the glistening hand slowly freed, dropping away from the ragged wrist.

This man, her husband, looked up, eyes dark knots in the rough bole of face. "I could not hold him," he gasped. "Wind or his own imagination. Once loose, I could not keep him here."

And then he looked away, back straining into the work of removing the tool that had failed him.

THE CHILD KILLER

All the mommas cry when the sackman comes.

It was the neighborhood fairytale, the nursery rhyme, the cautionary fable meant to scare the children just enough that they wouldn't stray too far, talk to strangers, or cross the wrong borders. He'd been hearing the stories for forty years, from the beginning of it all. And at one time the image of the large man (but not tall, not fat) with the huge, sure hands, walking the night streets with the voluminous gray sack across his back—a sack that sighed and cried, wriggled and shook as if there were small animals inside—had an almost romantic appeal. He felt flattered, and in fact the image hadn't been that far from the truth.

All the mommas cry when the sackman comes around. Back in the beginning, people minded their own business. Sackman. Like some sort of superhero. Now if people saw you with a sack like that they'd call the police. Even as all the mommas used the sackman to scare their kiddies out of misbehavior.

Now his hands shook, the way the children shook while he told them their special, their final, bedtime stories.

When he'd started it had been back after the war, and a sack wasn't all that unusual to see. Sometimes a sack was all a man had to carry what was important to him. And surely children were the most important things of all. Children were a comfort. Children were our future.

And he was the man whose task it was to murder the future.

Better get in before the sackman comes. Don't touch that if you don't want the sackman comin' round here! Better be good tonight or the old sackman may just up and take you for his dinner!

Back then, as now, what was important was the children he found. And no matter how good parents were, a few children confounded the purpose of these scary old cautionary tales. A few children were even more daring and reckless upon hearing of the sackman's activities. A few children were seemingly eager to fill his sack.

These were not bad children. The sackman had a hard time thinking of any of them as bad. Most often he thought it was, in fact, the best children who came into his sack, the ones with their heads all full of fairytales and visions of the future.

The sackman would send them all back to heaven if he could. This was impossible, of course, especially at his present age. Even if he recruited and shared his mission with thousands of like minded others, and surely they were out there, others cognizant of the need for such drastic measures, he couldn't send them all back. He knew it was impossible because they all needed a song or a story to send them on their way, much as small children about to fall into dreamland need a story to send them on their way, and he knew he would never be able to trust anyone else with such a grave responsibility.

The little girl with the red dress was once again in his park. She always wore the red dress and he had come to assume that she must have little else to wear. The dress had torn lace in the back and had faded almost to pink in the seat area. She always came to the park unsupervised. Sometimes her face was dirty, or bruised. He wondered, in part because of these things, if she understood yet that adults were monsters.

He would be very surprised if she had such an understanding. One of the stellar charms of children was that they could be so trusting. This quality never failed to move him. They could be lied to, cheated, and abused by half the adults of their acquaintance, and still the little angels continued to put their trust in these grown-up monsters.

"Where's your mother, dear?" he asked her again. She looked up at him solemnly, but said nothing. He patted her shoulder. He noticed with some inner disturbance that his hand trembled again. "Ah, at least someone has taught you not to speak to strangers. That's an important thing to remember, dear." He looked around and saw that no one else was around. He looked back down at her. "But I'm no stranger. You see, I'm just the grandfather you've never met, the kindly old man you've always dreamed about." Her eyes grew wider. "I can see that dream in your eyes right now, dear. I can see every little thing you're thinking. I know about little girls and little boys, you see."

Then he took her hand and she held on tightly, letting him know once and for all time that she was at last ready to go with him. They left the park hand-in-hand, in no particular hurry. He had been wearing makeup on all his trips to this park in another town, and he had been watching the child for weeks. Her calmness, her peace with him would allay all suspicions. Anyone who did see them together would assume he was an older relative taking the child to the park. If they wondered about anything it would be why the old man didn't buy the child a new dress. Obviously no one cared about this child. No one but the sackman.

She slid easily into the front passenger seat of his ancient, dark blue Buick. She was too short to see over the dashboard, but appeared fascinated by the old gauges beneath their highly-polished glass. He made sure she buckled the seat belt he had installed. His hands shook again (small animals in his sack) when the car wouldn't start, then calmed when the engine coughed into rough activity. He smiled down at the little girl. It warmed his old heart when she smiled back.

The drive back to his own home town was a long one, but the little girl sat through the trip patiently. At least someone had taught her manners. Now and then she would comment politely on the beauty of the drive. He had not lived in the actual town itself for many years, preferring the relative obscurity and safety of the mountains and lakes beyond. The old Buick struggled its way up the steep incline of the initial part of the drive, then relaxed as the highway leveled a few miles from his home. He had no idea how much longer the Buick could manage these trips. He supposed that once it failed his career as the sackman would be finished.

Not once on this long trip did this little girl ask where they were going. He took this to be clear evidence of a long pattern of deprivations. Normally he would have had to trot out any one of a dozen different fantasies in order to placate the little darling. Depending on the perceived needs, they were visiting long lost parents or friends, conducting a secret mission for the government, aiding a dying or injured relative, or visiting a castle, space ship, or miscellaneous wonderland. But the little girl asked no questions, so he was careful not to provide any answers.

When they finally arrived she jumped out and ran toward the house. "It's like a cave!" she exclaimed, and indeed it was.

More than half of the house had been built into a hollow carved into the mountainside.

Here comes the sackman, sweetheart, he thought as he followed her to the undersized front door. As always he had to stoop with the key in his trembling fist in order to let them inside.

"Wait here while I get the light," he said softly to the darkness. He reached overhead for the cord to the bulb. That was when she ran away into the shadows of his mountain home.

He was too startled to speak, reduced to gripping and ungripping the cotton light cord as if in a spasm. The bulb flickered into yellow dimness.

"Where? Are you!" he finally sputtered in rage. There was no answer from the shadows of his cave.

He waited by the door for a time, listening carefully the way the sackman was supposed to listen—the sackman who all the mommas said could detect a small child's heartbeat amongst all the other heartbeats in the deep dark woods—but he heard nothing. He felt suddenly exhausted, as if all the bright red blood had run out of him, and he was compelled to collapse into the overstuffed chair by the door—placed there years before for exactly these attacks of sudden fatigue. He could remember placing the chair here himself one day after a young boy of seven had run him practically to tatters in the surrounding woods. He could remember, too, how he had felt when he'd finally caught the boy (who, also tired, could only look up at the sackman with eyes the size of quarters), and telling the boy about the lands that lay beyond dreams, the countries where children had no bodies that puked and stank but instead travelled within beams of pure white light, had placed his huge rough hand over the small boy's face and with only the tiniest of disturbances—a cough and a squirm as if the lad were stirring within a bad dream—had sent him swiftly into that wondrous land.

But the sackman could not remember when he had grown so old.

"Little one!" he called, after catching his breath enough to say it softly, tenderly. "Come back to see your old grandpa, honey. We'll play hide-and-go-seek later. I promise." There was a distant giggle back in the dark far-off rooms of his house, but nothing more. The sackman bit into his lower lip until the blood spurted, and then he began to suck. He closed his eyes and stared at red circles in the darkness. When he at last opened them again, the giggles had started again. It had been a very long time since a giggle had been heard in his house.

To the casual observer, the sackman's front room was furnished unremarkably—the more obvious mementoes of all his children were displayed in the back rooms of the house, the chambers down under the cool mountainside, the shadowed places where the little girl in the red dress now laughed and hid.

"Are you Little Red Riding Hood? Is that who you've decided to be, my sweet?" Then the sackman howled his best wolf howl, an old wolf certainly, but without a doubt a huge, snarling horrific wolf it was. For the sackman had had much practice over the years playing the part of the wolf.

There was no answer and the sackman laughed as loudly as he had howled, and felt young again.

Then the sackman sucked some more of his own salty blood, smiled and looked around his front room, and saw:

A large pot he'd once upended over a small girl, four or five years but small for her age, the smallest child he'd ever had in his home. (Although not the smallest he'd ever sent back to heaven. Back during the fifties he'd sent back a half dozen babies who'd been sleeping in bassinets and on blankets in the park. All that had been required was something to distract the mothers. There'd been time for only the briefest of bedtime stories, but babies required very little, being half dream and parental anticipation already.) He'd kept her in that pot until she'd been quite convinced he was going to cook her, so that she was almost relieved when finally it was his hands that sent her on her way.

A worn-out sofa with oversized cushions. For three full days he'd once lain on that sofa, taking his meals there, even relieving himself into a hole in the worn-out upholstery when he couldn't hold it any longer. A visitor would have seen a smelly, sickly old man lying there, perhaps breathing his last. A visitor never would have guessed a skinny ten-year-old boy lay underneath those cushions, the life squeezing out of his semi-conscious body an hour at a time.

A tall kitchen trash can over in the corner once contained twin six-year-olds tied together, face-to-face. He'd used both his huge hands to send them on their way, at the same time, providing them with a joint fairytale, a shared dream, making sure that they might look into each other's eyes as they began their long journey back. Now he could not remember if they had been boys or girls.

The fireplace along a side wall appeared much too large for the room, but otherwise was unremarkable in every way. It didn't even sport a rudimentary mantel. But more than once it had contained giant logs of newspaper wrapped in wire, each with a small child completely hidden inside. He would never have considered burning a precious child, although he had been content to let them think so. It was all part of his game, and their personalized fairytale.

The sackman had no illusions about what an outsider might think if he or she (some matronly social worker, going house to house in behalf of children's welfare) stumbled onto his doings, or witnessed any of the games he played with the children. He had given up hope for understanding many years ago, although he was convinced there were hundreds of people like him in the world who might appreciate his mission. Who understood that children were lied to, made to anticipate an adulthood full of promise and dream, when all the time the promises and dreams ended with the onset of puberty. The life of an adult was made putrid by constant disappointments and betrayals. Only a child, a mere eyeblink out of heaven's embrace, could glimpse glory. But after the development of the sexual organs and the accompanying desires it was as if they had been blinded, never to see the brilliant light of heaven again.

The sackman loved children, and envied them. So what better way might he show that love than to send them back to heaven where they belonged, where they would truly want to go if they only had the understanding ironically wasted on adults?

From the sackman's under-the-mountain rooms, where much more obvious secrets and mementoes of his career were kept, came the sound of footsteps and giggles and can't-catch-mes. Surely it was time for this particular child's game to end, and her final fairytale to begin.

The sackman's eyes were old, but they were still the eyes of the sackman. Who sees everything, child, so just you watch out!

Don't let him catch you out tonight! He could still see clearly where this one little girl had been.

One of the giant clothes closets off the east hallway had been opened up, and decades of children's dresses and shorts, pants and socks and shirts and underwear had spilled out, some of it vomit- or blood- or other-stained, all of it precious reminders of the children he had known and loved into heaven. He stopped for a moment and tried to pick some of these up, trying to match pieces of outfits, trying to match clothing with vague, frightened, then peacefully sleeping little faces, but it was an impossible task. There were too many dead children spilt here, too many tiny ghosts struggling into these scattered outfits every morning. With tears washing his face he cast them aside and called "Darling!" and "Sweetheart!" and even "Grandchild!", careful to keep the growing rage out of his voice, but all he heard was the distant laughter, the small feet running from room to room, crashing through all the doors of his life.

"Baby!" he shouted, kicking the piles of torn little body parts aside. "Baby, come here!" and pounded his feet into the floor to make a Giant's footsteps guaranteed to terrify even the bravest Jack.

He could hear her somewhere just ahead of him now, racing in and out of the numerous dimly-lit or dark rooms that spread far under the mountainside.

In one room numerous toys, furred in greasy dust so that they appeared half-animal, half-appliance, had been removed from their storage shelves and scattered about the floor. The hands that had once played with these played with toys of pure light now. But it still angered him that they'd been touched, perhaps even damaged, without his permission. "Nice little girls ask before playing with another's things!" he shouted into the darkness. But the darkness continued to run and cast its laughter back at the sackman.

He inhaled deeply of the cold, musty air of these backrooms, these storage chambers of his past, this air redolent of ten thousand children's screams, children's fear sweat, breath stink, and blood. He felt the air lengthening his stride, putting the power back into his huge hands. With each inhalation, with each new insult from this anonymous little girl, he felt as if his mass and muscle were increasing, his old man's fatigue draining away, until by the time he reached the farthest, deepest rooms, he'd become convinced that he was the sackman of forty years ago, the terror of children and their parents for three states around.

The doors to wall cabinets had been thrown open, countless pairs of small children's glasses spilled out onto the hard gray rock floors. Some were shattered, some had their frames bent and twisted. He gathered them up by the handfuls and piled them on a nearby table alongside two miniature prosthetic arms, a prosthetic leg, and several cigar boxes full of dental appliances. One pair of glasses had snagged on his black coat sleeve—he picked it off and examined it, recalling how he'd always been amazed by these prescription lenses for children, how small they were, as if fitted for dolls or ventriloquist dummies. He tried to wedge the glasses over his own eyes, and his eyes seemed larger than the lenses themselves (The sackman has great big saucers for eyes. He can see you wherever you go. He always knows what you're doing.) From beneath the small lenses he could feel the darkness pushing down in a spiraling rush, a huge face suddenly looming over him, greasy lips parting to show dancing teeth as the sackman began his recital of the final fairytale.

He jerked the glasses off and threw them across the room. When he turned, he could hear the footsteps in an adjacent room. Far too many footsteps.

At the next room he opened the heavy door (heavy as stone the door to his home) and was greeted by a shower of children's shoes: high-tops, sneakers, black patent leathers, flip-flops, leather sandals, Buster Browns, Oxfords, Minnie Mouse slippers, skates, tap shoes—as they fell from upended shelves and splintered apple crates. He screamed a not very sackman-like scream as the shoes tumbled over his head and shoulders, soles slapping a staccato as if in footless dance. Yet even as he screamed he could still hear the high hysterical giggles of sung accompaniment gradually fading into the rooms beyond.

The sackman kicked his way through the knee-high piles of shoes into the disarray of the next room (crude children's drawings of knifings, stranglings, and decapitations littering the floor like gigantic leaves), and then the next (piles of naked dolls, dark bruises and red tears painted on their faces), and the next (volumes of candid photographs of dead children, taken immediately before and after their last moments in this loathsome world, ripped and torn and tossed up into the cold drafts like confetti).

"Enough! Enough!" he cried, feeling uncomfortably like a timid schoolmaster who's lost control of his class. "It's fairytale time! You like fairytales don't you?"

"Oh yes oh yes," she murmured from not so far away.

He turned his head and staggered in fatigue, suddenly feeling old again. He was alarmed to find that he could not quite catch his breath. "Just let me... let me catch my breath... please..."

"No! I want my storyyyyyyy!" The little girl appeared at the end of the hall swathed in sheets stained maroon from dried blood (she's been in my private bedroom!) and started running toward him. Startled, the sackman lost his balance and fell to the floor. As her laughter reached for an ever higher pitch he lifted his huge, child-killer hands to protect his face.

She pulled a round, flat object—larger than a dinner plate—out of the bloody sheet and threw it at him much in the manner of a Frisbee. He recognized it as a trophy he had made for himself many years ago. It broke into pieces on his arms, cutting and (gnawing) into his tender old flesh. He groped for the pieces on the floor and came up with handfuls of his children's precious baby teeth which had been glued on to the trophy as decoration, and finally the larger pieces—part of what had once been a beautiful lily glued together from thousands of such teeth.

"You little bitch!" He scrambled to his feet and lunged toward her ghostly form. She backed away and backed away, tittering and chuckling, the snot running from her nose as she grew more hysterical. He almost had her within his grasp when she turned and ran. He lunged again, pulled the rotting sheet from her body, and crashed through the next door, huge splinters piercing his face, ramming through the loose flesh on his arms, hammering through knuckles and the webbing by each thumb, working themselves deep into his belly as if conscious and determinedly murderous.

They were in his secret bedroom (my heart!). The little girl in the tattered red dress jumped up and down on his bed, picking up the old blood-stained covers and tossing them into the far corners of the room. Oh, she's found my secret heart!

"Can't catch me now can't catch me now..." she chanted breathlessly. The sackman could see that she had smeared herself with the rancid fluids of corruption from his bottle collection underneath the bed (even he would not have done such a thing—for him it was always enough just to know they were there beneath his reclining form). She stuck out her tongue demonically.

He tried to get up off the floor but each movement brought the sharp splinters deeper into his body. He knew she had done real damage to him because he had a vague sensation of soft, secret things tearing away inside him. But strangely enough all his rage had fled him. He felt too old for such anger. His mission, as always, was most important now. "Child . . . sweet child," he implored weakly. "It is time for your story. Surely you want your story? Hurry! While I still have the strength..."

"I love stories," she said quietly, but not looking at him. Instead she looked around at his bedroom. She was the only person besides him ever to be in his bedroom.

"All children love stories," he replied. "Especially bedtime stories." But still she wouldn't look at him, intent on the walls of his bedroom, walls decorated with all the collages of his universe he had constructed over the years:

Along the bottoms of the walls were countless pictures of children, but with heads, arms, legs removed, eyes cut from their sockets, genitalia snipped and glued to their foreheads, ears and eyes glued over small, immature breasts, tongues affixed to the bottoms of tiny feet. The children were stacked and piled until they made a terrible weight at the bottom of each collage, where sometimes the paper was cut, and passages were made to other collages which were even more crowded with segmented children. Brown and red offal and old excrement had been smeared in and out of these segments for this was the world, this was the everyday ground human beings walked on, slept on, rutted and conducted their commerce on.

Arranged at eye level were various upright figures: roaches and mayflies and lizards and centipedes and dark birds. These were built from shapes outlined in charcoal, cut out, then arranged to construct the desired form, or sometimes they were photographs of world leaders—Stalin, Reagan, Thatcher, De Gaulle—with bits cut away until the hidden creature had been uncovered. Each held a knife or an axe or a sack or a pair of scissors, for these were the harvesters. Here and there their barbed legs or wings reached down into the collages below to snare a child and free it from its own corporeal filth.

But above eye level, further than a child could reach on his or her own, was heaven, where the walls had been scrubbed until they were practically no color at all. There the sackman had pasted small bits of paper. And on each piece of paper was scribbled the final words of a child he had personally harvested, liberated, discorporated, sent back. All the no please momma stop daddy yes I'll be good your eyes why your hands can't why Why WHYs, and prayers far more obscure than he had ever heard.

"You're a bad man," the little girl said, and grinned. A stare into the brilliance of the little girl's grin and the sackman felt bathed in ice.

"No. No, honey. I'm the very best of men. You'll understand that after I've told you your story."

Then he grabbed her by one scuffed tennis shoe and began pulling her off the bed and into his bloody, splintered embrace.

The little girl squealed as if it were a game. The sackman began to relax, because it was a game, the most important game she would ever play.

"This is a story about a little girl in a red dress," he whispered from bloody lips.

"And you're making it lots more redder," she said moistly into his ear.

"Who never wanted to grow up," he continued.

"I wouldn't want to be like you!" She giggled.

"Stop interrupting," he said firmly, and she snuggled closer to him, soaking herself completely in the blood seeping from his enormous lap. "Now that might sound strange to some people, not wanting to grow up, but this little girl was very smart, you see..."

"Very smart," she interrupted, but he ignored her.

"... because she'd known lots of grownups in her time, and she'd learned what awful beasts grownups could be. They'd forgotten what it had been like to be a child, how very hard it had been, and it was this absent mindedness that had turned all the grownups into scaly, putrid monsters!"

"Really?" the little girl asked, wide-eyed.

"Really."

"So what did she do?" She seemed genuinely interested. He'd never had a child so relaxed in his arms before, despite all that had happened. Perhaps this would be the one child who really understood. Perhaps she would go easily, with no need for a struggle. He stretched his fingers and spread his huge hands (watch out! watch out!). He brought his fingers closer to her neck (when he comes), closer to her tiny, grape-shaped eyes (when the sackman comes).

"What did she do, you ask? Why, she visited the sackman, of course."

"That was stupid!" she squealed, and rammed a long splinter of wood up through his belly until it found the sackman's chest.

As the sackman felt himself falling into bits and pieces, his legs tumbling one way, his arms and belly another, he tried to think of the word he'd want the little girl to write down for pasting into his sackman heaven.

She let him pull her closer. He could see her leaning over his lips with an anxious expression on her face, ready to hear and record. He closed his eyes and opened his mouth, and felt her eager fingers tearing at his tongue.

FRIDAY NIGHTS

The first visits had been straightforward enough. He'd started going there to meet women. His wife had been gone almost a year and the women at work seemed too old for him. It had been a long time since he'd thought about how a woman might see him, the kind of messages he sent out. Did he even send out messages? Everyone did, according to the articles in the women's magazines, which had become his secret vice. After Clara left and he'd been so stupefied by the whole thing he'd thought reading them might help him understand—certainly she'd spent more time reading them than telling him the truth.

"How To Tell Your Man What He's Doing Wrong." He wondered if she'd read that one and if so, why she hadn't followed its recommendations. Maybe she'd decided he wasn't worth the aggravation.

He didn't go to Jack's to meet women anymore. To see them, yes, to smell them. To be in their presence.

"I tell you, the women go crazy there!" Mark had thought going to Jack's was the best thing Jim could do. If he wanted to meet women, and what man didn't? "It's either Jack's, or a church, or even better a funeral at a church. But Jack's is where they really let loose, where they really get crazy." Jim didn't actually want a crazy woman, but maybe momentary insanity was as good an ice-breaker as any.

Dating had this vaguely disturbing terminology—breaking the ice, sending messages. It seemed strangely science fictional, contact between two alien species. He couldn't imagine his parents being this way, but he couldn't remember much communicating taking place there, either. Maybe it had always been this way and he'd just never noticed before. Marriage protected you from the real terrors of relationships.

"I don't think I've danced in years—how about you?"

The fellow—about his age, maybe a little older—made this opening statement and waited for an answer. Some people might have been tempted to make fun of him, but Jim wasn't one of them. Something had to be said first and perhaps this was as good a thing to say as any. The first thing you said in any relationship had little long-lasting meaning. The first thing you said could even be a lie. The woman's eyes moved slightly down and up again, almost imperceptibly, a sizing up and a conclusion. She had to determine if this guy was at least in the ballpark and if she didn't do it now she might be stuck with a major incompatibility for half the evening. Not as cruel as it sounded—she was doing both of them a favor.

At their age the standards were a bit looser, of course. At their age even a man years out of shape might interest an ex-prom queen.

The woman smiled, always an encouraging sign. Good for you, fellow, Jim thought. Good for you.

Mark had stopped coming to Jack's several years ago, having found a girlfriend and then moving to Seattle where he thought people were friendlier. "It's the rain and the gloom that brings people closer together." Mark had theories about all varieties of human behavior. Nothing strange about that, of course. Theories were pretty much all most of us knew about being human. Mark's problem was that his theories were a bit further off the beam than most, and his need too obvious, too painful to observe.

"Look at them," Mark had said, gesturing toward the variety of women crowding the dance floor, heads drifting up and down. "It's just like sex."

Jim had understood then that Mark knew very little about sex. Not that Jim was an expert. But during the course of his eight-year marriage to Clara they had had three different kinds of sex, all of them authentic in their own way.

Initially there had been the pretense of passion and exhaustion while they attempted to understand the real passion that lay beneath: the bellies sucked in, the dramatic breathing and groaning and sudden cries, the collapse at the end and the various half-true declarations, and the final separate awarenesses that they had not quite found the complete release they'd always dreamed of, but they knew it was there.

Then there had been two years or so of slow comforts, a joining in weariness at the end of the day, and the easing out of tears and the almost-desperate final embraces. These were the times Jim would always recall with fondness, and think of as love.

And then there came that last year of marathon exhaustion, as if both of them were in training for the new life to come, using each other like exercise equipment, a race into oblivion before turning over and falling asleep.

Mark had no idea of any of this. All he had seen out on the dance floor were tides of women. It had been ladies' choice and the ladies had chosen to move together as one, not so much displaying themselves as keeping themselves alive, for to stand unmoving when you could still hear the music was to harden into something ailing and sad.

"I'm on the road a lot," the tall sandy-haired man said to the woman he was dancing with.

Jim's partner was a short, pale woman several years his

senior. She never smiled; dancing with strange men was a serious assignment for her, self-assigned or based on recommendations from friends or a therapist.

"That must be very interesting, to be able to travel all the time," the woman in the red dress replied.

The man laughed a little too hard, on the edge of being offensive. Jim saw the woman frown. Do you think I'm stupid? was in her face but she didn't voice it.

The man might have told her about his time on the road because it was the only thing he could think of to say or because he wanted to quickly signal his lack of interest in a long-term relationship. The woman's assessment that this information was somehow interesting was probably a lie, but it gave her an excuse to express a desire to travel which might have also encouraged further conversation about distant places and times. The man might have truly found her to be stupid, or boring, but more than likely he had laughed as an anxiety release. Jim heard more nervous laughter out on the dance floor than in any other setting he could think of.

Some time during this assessment Jim had changed partners, without being fully aware that it was happening. The woman across from him now didn't look at him, one of the many advantages of a fast song. Fast songs also afforded the opportunity to release sexual tension, an important mechanism for avoiding violence when there were a lot of young single men in the club at one time.

"She did you a favor, leaving you," Mark had said that first night at the club, a little too loudly. "At least now you can get yourself good and properly laid." Jim had barely controlled the urge to punch him. He had never punched anyone, and now it seemed appropriate, dealing with a fool. But he didn't.

Next to him an older man wearing red suspenders gyrated to music Jim suspected he had never heard before. Jim was bad with ages—people his exact same age always looked much older or much younger to him—but he thought the man must be over sixty. He danced with a woman who might have been his daughter, but Jim didn't think so. Unattached women at Jack's tended be quite democratic with their dance partners. To be otherwise might send an unwanted message about their motivations for being there. The guy appeared to be using the music as an excuse for exercise, holding off death as best he could. Jim wondered if he had any romantic interest in the younger woman. It was doubtful, but you could never tell for sure.

For ten years Jim had been coming to Jack's for "oldies" on Friday nights. The mix of ages and singles versus marrieds had stayed pretty constant during that time. But ten years had been long enough for the newer music, played from eleven to midnight each evening, to become part of the oldies musical rotation in subsequent years. At this point the regulars usually started losing interest, most of them eventually dropping out altogether. Jim often wondered what they did on their Fridays instead. He suspected that a particular sort of sad self-consciousness had come into the experience for them as the music aged, preventing them from completely abandoning themselves to the music.

Jim felt himself immune to sadness. He'd long ago concluded it was like checking into a bad hotel room. You just went down to see the manager and requested another. No sense being anxious over a chance encounter—what was life beyond a series of chance encounters?

This evening few smiled out on the dance floor. Either they had their minds on other activities or they were so focused on doing the current activity correctly they forgot how their faces should appear. A smile wasn't always best, of course, but it was a convenient default.

Explaining some new intention to exercise or diet or tan or purchase or hairdo or make-up style, Clara used to say, "After all, your body is a vessel." Jim hadn't always taken the statement seriously: she threw it away too easily. He supposed she didn't really understand it herself, despite the fact that she'd always been obsessed with her "vessel": keeping it fit and clean, adorning it to fit the times and her mood, reshaping it as a final, desperate measure when it no longer resembled what it used to be.

Out on the dance floor these vessels bobbed up and down on a tide of rhythmic noise, mouths and minds open, receptive to whatever filling might be available: jobs, partners, a life in the suburbs, a vacation on the beach, a trip out of town, a grope in the back of a shiny black van. Like dancers at some voodoo ceremony, waiting for a random god to possess them. No matter what people said about their lives, none of it was true in any sort of fundamental way. Even your name, he thought, is arbitrary. A physical body dancing in the tide is as close to what you are as anything.

A dark-haired woman with a white streak like a curved knife blade above one ear stood at the edge of the floor watching him. He looked around. Apparently at some point his dance partner had disappeared, and at the moment he had no memory of what she had looked like. He wondered how long he'd been dancing by himself, thinking it should embarrass him, but it did not. He had seen people—mostly drunk, mostly women but not always—dance by themselves before.

He stopped dancing, but not so abruptly as to draw additional attention. He found himself swaying rhythmically as he moved off the floor. He couldn't help himself. The woman continued to stare at him. He thought at first to avoid her—the bold ones almost invariably became drunk and irritating—but found himself exiting the dance area close to where she stood. Maybe it was the hair. She looked more curious than anything. Jim didn't think he'd ever seen her here before.

"You seem to have lost your partner." She smiled, letting him know the comment was friendly.

He smiled back. He seldom went long without a dance partner, but smiling was something he rarely did. The small events of a life were simply not that amusing. "And you don't appear to have a partner."

The woman began to dance, moving slowly out to the floor,

and after a brief hesitation he joined her. He thought it staged and somewhat silly, but it was almost closing time, and he had been there for hours, so why fight it—she seemed like a nice lady.

Still, he would have just finished this little dance and said his goodnights if she hadn't stared at him the way she did, eyes wide open like a curious child's, taking in every detail of his face and expression. If only to distract her he remarked, "I don't believe I've seen you in here before."

"I buried my husband two weeks ago," she said, as if that were a logical reply.

"I'm sorry."

"Oh, well, I'm sorry. It's not something to share in a first meeting."

"It's this place. People find themselves saying strange things." But of course she wasn't one of those people. She was simply being perfectly honest. Looking at her, he suspected she was barely capable of anything else.

"You must have been coming here for awhile." Women had said this to him before, of course, but it bridled him a bit because he could tell she expected an honest answer.

"Years," he said. "But it hasn't improved my dancing any."

And she laughed a genuine laugh, which made her seem too vulnerable to be in a place like this, and he began wondering how it would feel to hurt her.

After Jack's closed they walked outside together. This was not something Jim usually did. Usually he ignored all invitations spoken or implied, said his goodbyes, and returned to his apartment alone. It was a small place, hardly big enough for his own concerns.

But when Helen asked him outside for a walk ("It's strange, I'm not sleepy at all.") he had said yes. Of course. And had allowed her to take his arm.

There was really no place to walk outside Jack's. The building was off an access road by a major north/south interstate, the hot air rank with oil and diesel fumes. Every few minutes a tractor trailer would blow its air horn and rumble past on its way to a nearby depot. Jack's neighbors were other bars and run-down hotels, a storage business and a lumber yard. Very little grass grew above the curbs, but even here an effort at landscaping had been made with rounded, white-painted stones and the occasional flower bed. Jack wondered what kind of person put out such effort, when it had no chance of being noticed. But at least it gave them a place to walk off the pavement. Property fences ended a few feet from the curbs, so that there was a continuous strip of this poor vegetation and painful landscaping. By including the occasional tree used to obscure side entrances or other semi-private features, an optimistic imagination might envision a parkway in the early morning darkness. He suspected that to be her particular fantasy—she seemed far too at ease for his own comfort.

"It's probably unseemly for me to go out so soon, but he was ill for such a long time, and I was so afraid I'd turn into one of those women."

"Those women?"

"Women who stay at home the rest of their lives, or until they can't stand it anymore and come out of hiding just to make the worst possible choices."

"Is that important to you, making good choices?"

She stopped and gripped his hand tighter, looking up at him. When had they started holding hands? He had no idea. Like school kids. He wanted to get his hand away from her, but didn't want to break the curious tone of the evening. "Probably not as important as it should be," she said.

They walked more than an hour with hands linked at the edge of the curb until awkward footing gave him the opportunity to withdraw his hand. He watched her as she looked up at the lightening sky, at the shadowed trucks passing on the highway, smiling as if she were out on some great adventure, some sort of safari, and such naiveté repelled him. Clearly, she hadn't the slightest grasp of the true dangers of the world. She was a murder waiting to happen.

"You're not married, are you?"

He looked at her in surprise. "No, of course not, why would you think…"

"I'm sorry. I didn't mean to offend you. I just had this sudden thought, 'Maybe he's married.' I don't know why."

Actually, the fact that she thought to ask the question raised her in his estimation. He briefly considered answering 'yes,' curious what her response might be. "No. My wife left me years ago."

"Oh! I'm so sorry."

"No, no. Like I said, it's been years."

She said nothing for awhile, concentrating on her feet. A shiny, fifties-style diner gleamed from the lot ahead, but after that there was nothing but weeds and ill-kept road for a mile or more. Such stupidity, he thought. Women were killed in places like this. Bodies were dumped. So much unnecessary waste in the world. So much lost potential.

"I was married for years," she said quietly. "Happily, but it was almost all I ever knew. Each day must be like an adventure for you. You must feel like you could do anything."

She was giving him every opportunity to impress her with his lies. So this was the way it happened. This was the way nice, lonely women got themselves killed. "Right now," he said, "I suppose I could do anything. Just to see how it would feel."

"Oh, I can tell you have a great deal of potential. I could see that from the beginning."

"Just to feel anything, really. People go to such lengths sometimes. Just to feel something."

"That's so true. And all the time it's right there in front of you."

"The opportunity is there. No one would know."

"Absolutely. No one knows how any of us feels." She grabbed his forearm and looked up into his eyes. "But I believe you can tell a lot about a person, if you just look at them, really look at them."

He returned her gaze, trying to let something come through

that would beam down from his eyes and brand her. Not a warning exactly. Perhaps just a glimpse at what the human heart is truly capable of. But she hadn't a clue. "I can tell that you're a very sensitive person," she said, misinterpreting everything. "Let me buy you breakfast."

They sat together in the diner for over an hour eating their slow breakfast. Everything was too bright: the chrome trim around the walls and tables, the ghastly intensity of the fluorescents, the early sap of the day rising out of unpromising concrete to fill the air with brilliance. Her face. Older than his, he thought, much older than she'd seemed in the dark. But he was so bad with ages, he reminded himself. It suddenly occurred to him that he might look old. That's why she had taken such a risk, gone walking out into the darkness with a less-than-perfect stranger. Because he'd looked too old to do her any harm.

Make-up had caked near her eyes and at the left corner of her mouth. He could see now that she used a little too much lipstick. And something was wrong with her eye shadow: she looked more bruised than seductive. No doubt during the walk here she had perspired, and the make-up had run a bit. Or maybe it had happened during dancing. Some women perspired more, but he hadn't been aware of her dancing with anyone other than him. It had been as if she'd been waiting. Waiting for someone like him. Her murderer.

Not that he had ever murdered anyone. He'd never even punched anyone. His previous murders had been strictly academic. He was like one of those fellows who played entire games of chess in his head, and never went near a board and pieces. She might have been his first.

But the woman didn't know how to put make-up on anymore. That was it, wasn't it? She'd come to Jack's like this, and he hadn't known because of the dim lighting.

She smiled up at him. A small bit of congealed egg clung to one powder- and grease-smeared cheek. He picked up a napkin and dipped one corner into his water glass. "Here," he said. "Here. You've got something on you. Let me." And he reached over, and she sat still as a daughter while he smoothed the place by her mouth, and blended her eye shadow, and gently removed the food clinging to her cheek. "Like a picture," he said. "Like a pretty picture."

She held his hand. "You're a good man," she said, knowing absolutely nothing about him, and it hurt him so to hear, and he could feel the anger coming as if from a great distance.

"Excuse me," he said. "I have to go the bathroom." He got up and walked to the back of the restaurant, and the hall that led to the restrooms, and he walked past the restrooms and out the back door, away from his first real victim.

The morning was hot and dusty and he was still dressed in his best outfit, the black shirt and slacks and the thin silver tie. He walked through the weed and dirt lot behind the diner and wedged himself through a break in the fence.

He walked down several blocks of bad pavement, poor houses and trashy yards. Ahead of him was a church, and a number of people in nice dresses and suits stood beneath an awning in the graveyard. He came as close to the funeral as he could. No one noticed him. Until a woman's voice, slightly to his left and behind. "I see I'm not the only one who's late," she whispered, and drew closer, stepping beside him so they looked like a couple who had traveled here together to pay their respects.

"I didn't know her that well," she said softly. "But I hear she was just a wonderful woman."

He tried to look beyond the perfect make-up job, and could not. "I didn't know her at all," he said.

"I know exactly what you mean," she replied, completely misunderstanding him, not knowing anything that would help her through the next few hours.

SQUEEZER

“You look like you deserve a hug,” Anita said, again, as she had said every time Jefferson ran into her. Only this time they were alone, late at night in the park across the street from the movie theater. There wasn’t the crowd of people around she had always seemed to require. The crowd whose individual members looked so fondly at Anita’s heartfelt expressions of her humanity. “I think you do! I think you do deserve a hug today!”

When there was a crowd Jefferson could avoid her; he could fade into that large and unmanageable, unhuggable crowd.

But here there were no witnesses. The last show at the theatre had been an hour ago; Jefferson had hung around in the park because he liked the dark and the relative emptiness of late night. He had not expected to see Anita here—he supposed she was returning from some late night hugging session.

She looked at him intently and seemed disturbed by what she saw. But then she had never seen Jefferson late at night, with no one else around. She started to pass him, confirming finally for him that these offers of hugs had become merely formal, required greeting for her, and had no conviction behind them at all.

Tonight Jefferson would have none of that. It was dark and there was no one else around, and he had not touched, much less held, anyone in months. His skin felt dead, a brittle carapace for his nerves. His bones ached as if riddled with holes. He had a need to touch someone else's life, and if not their life at least their desperation, which for him was much the same thing.

He stepped forward into her body and offered himself up to her embrace. She hesitated at first, stiffened as if there were something wrong with his skin, as if she had found something repulsive in the feel of him, but then she whispered "Oh, sweetie..." with a heavy exhalation, as if a hope had at last been realized, and wrapped her arms around him, her legs and hips seeming to stretch, as if she would envelope him completely if she could.

Jefferson held fast to her, at first in a familiar desperation, using her to anchor himself to the remaining tatters of his sense of reality. Then he increased the firmness of this embrace as he felt more and more in control of himself and of his situation. This young woman said she believed in touching, had in fact made hugging a credo, an entire belief system. But he sincerely doubted she understood touching at all. He believed a true touch between human beings to be impossible. But it was that impossibility which made it seem so essential. In fact, his embrace became so strong that the surface area of his arms and hands seemed to increase dramatically, impossibly, so that his grip covered every inch of her flesh, every square inch of her life, so that he could feel her increasingly harsh breathing beneath his touch, her pores opening in panic beneath his touch, releasing the oils and toxins all lives give off as they are winding down, as he squeezed and squeezed in an attempt to touch the life within her, to know that life at the level of his fingertips.

When at last he felt the spasms beneath his hands, the last swift jerks of her body, he looked down at her steady gaze, her lips sheened with a red froth as they dropped back as if to take his mouth in a final kiss, and he wondered at what he had done.

• • •

Jefferson would think of Anita many times after that. She became more to him than merely a first love, more like his first encounter with the sweet pulse which drove life itself. She was his first bride, and although even then he knew there would be many others, surely there could never be another to surpass the feel or the taste of his sweet Anita.

She became the standard by which he judged other women, by which he imagined them. And during the months which followed he would imagine many women in his arms.

Marie was someone he followed for weeks before finally arranging their "accidental" meeting. She cleaned several of the larger houses in the neighborhood, arriving at the corner by bus each morning around nine, and normally departing the same way about two PM. She was short, slight, brunette; some might have called her "ethereal." It was easy for him to imagine her dissolving completely under the persistent press of his arms.

She ate lunch every day at the Blue Ribbon Diner. After several days of watching her, Jefferson adopted the same habit, choosing a table to the side, only a few feet away.

She ate a great deal for such a small person. He wondered where she put it all.

He dreamed of squeezing the food back out of her, years of it unused and simply waiting for him to empty her with his embrace. All that untapped energy, all that unused life.

Once or twice she glanced in his direction and smiled. He felt his arm muscles tense, his chest suddenly swelling with an emptiness.

At last came a day he chose to come late, after the lunch rush was well under way. As always, there was the empty chair at her table.

"May I?" He smiled widely, and he could feel a strain in his empty belly.

"Sure…I don't mind," she said, as if it mattered. "I see you here all the time."

"You always make the food taste better," he said. He made

himself say it without blushing. Anita had given him just that kind of confidence.

She looked at him with a slightly startled expression, then laughed out loud, presumably at the audacity of his compliment. But she still smiled at him. She nodded and hid her eyes. Obviously he had pleased her.

Over the next few weeks Jefferson was careful when and where and how he touched her. He was courting her embrace, in fact, and had to make his moves cautiously, despite his sometimes overwhelming desire to bury her under his hands. She seemed anxious for more as well, and now and then he had to stop her from moving his hand to where he was not yet ready to be.

"Kiss me," she whispered late one afternoon, long after her regular bus had left. She had led him to a quiet corner of the park, surrounded by broad shrubbery. "Please... don't be shy." Her breath was full and warm against his face. His fingers itched to enter her lips and meet that breath at its source.

"Not now. Patience..." he whispered back at her. Her back stiffened under his hand. He wanted badly to press into these hardened muscles—how firm she had become through her labors, so wonderfully fit that he could have written testimonials to the physical efficacy of housework for the modern woman's figure—but he had to pull his hand away instead.

"Just... forget it!" She stood up and started away.

He was afraid he had waited too long. He leaped up and ran behind her, grabbing her around the waist and turning her, and holding on with eyes squeezed shut as his lips suddenly opened and he said, in a voice that sounded so much like Anita, whom he had squeezed into the empty spaces inside himself that long ago night, "You look like you need a hug."

He was surprised to find that the tighter he squeezed her, the tighter she squeezed back.

"Hold me," she whispered with ragged breath. "Hold me tight."

And he did. He held her because she wanted him to hold

her—that was always the best way. Like everyone else in the world she needed to be held. The flesh of the human body clung all too tightly to its solitary bones. The mixing of flesh, the joining of individual bodies, was illusory, and always promised far more than was delivered. Make love for hours with even remarkable talent and passion and you still finished the evening spent and alone within your own sweat-slicked, shivering hide, your own thoughts hidden and untouchable from the other beside you in your bed. All you could do was hold, and squeeze, and imagine a bonding of skin to skin which could not happen no matter how desperately you squeezed.

"Too tight, honey. Too tight," she said between clenched teeth trying to resemble a smile. But Jefferson could see the fear and confusion in her eyes. He moved his hands to her neck and her face and squeezed some more, and was amazed at the relaxation forced into her muscles, the redness and then the pallor that came to her cheeks, and as he squeezed he imagined her moving into the too-rigid outlines of his body, and he could almost hear the endless conversations they might have inside himself.

Blue shaded her eyes as in his mind his body opened lengthwise, like a huge vertical mouth, and took her in, and swallowed her up, and used her to assuage its loneliness.

Carol came into his life with a small child, Jenny, who was as beautiful as Carol herself, perhaps more so. At first Jefferson thought that the existence of this child must necessarily preclude his having any sort of relationship with Carol. For children frightened him. They always had. In part, he knew, this was because of the great delicacy of their bodies. It was hard for Jefferson to accept that such delicate bodies could survive. You couldn't help loving small children, certainly—their physical vulnerability made it inevitable. But that just made them all the more threatening, actually. They looked up at you with eyes filled with trust, and a mock-intelligence which suggested that they knew how you felt, that they were human beings as well, but their freakish vulnerability made that a lie. Their dwarfed, frail bodies were a joke, a hideous satire of the solitary death we each must face.

And yet for all his understanding, Jefferson was completely seduced by this little girl.

"Buy me a doll, please, Uncle Jeff?"

He wanted to ask her what she wanted it for, perhaps for companionship—she looked so much the doll herself, but he knew better than to say something others might think strange. "Your momma's going to think I spoil you." He made himself grin.

"Oh, spoil me, spoil me!" She laughed and gave him a hug.

"So you want a hug, huh?" he said into her blonde curls smelling of soap.

She pushed away and looked at him solemnly. Then nodded slowly, her eyes fixed on his.

He bent over and wrapped himself around her. But formally, with little pressure. It wasn't a real hug at all, the way he defined the word, but it appeared to satisfy her. She laid her small, all-too-crushable skull on his shoulder.

"Hugs are nice," she said softly.

"Hugs are all that really mean anything," he said. "Don't ever forget that."

"Well, I'd certainly agree with that," Carol said from the doorway. Jefferson looked through the yellow nimbus of Jenny's hair into Carol's smiling face.

"Jealous?" he asked, and made himself grin.

Carol strolled across the room toward them, the lines of her body flowing down and curving around him as she gathered him to her. "Oh, you bet," she breathed into his ear, and he wanted to pull away, so tightly she pulled on him, and so firmly her little girl still held on to his waist, a desperation with which he was so intimately familiar.

But he did not pull back, instead squeezing her in return,

although not as tightly as he was ultimately capable of squeezing.

The day was to be spent at a roadside carnival, a place where they could scream and fear for their lives without fully believing in that fear. It was one of Jefferson's favorite spots. Carol had been hesitant to go but Jenny was eager, typically with more enthusiasm than understanding. "You'll think you're going to die," he whispered to the little girl. "But then you don't. It's quite a surprise, really. I hope you won't be disappointed."

She nodded and watched his eyes solemnly.

The roadside carnival had been set up alongside Wildcat Wrecks, the oldest auto salvage yard in the region. This seemed so appropriate to Jefferson it practically took his breath away. The county commissioners had condemned it several times but at the last minute the owners always came up with some measure to avoid the action. Twisted wrecks and crushed cars were stacked into occasional mountains a dozen feet high, waiting for years sometimes until the price of scrap reached levels the owners thought acceptable, the sides of these precipices buttressed with piles of stone and miscellaneous rusted steel debris.

Jefferson thought of these automobiles as "people cans," a private little joke he had never shared with anyone. It was a wonder anyone ever survived their trips down the highway. The rides at the carnival pretended to be people cans as well, but he supposed they were in fact much safer.

On the roller coaster, in mock fear but in a truthfully passionate embrace, he almost squeezed Carol to death. Jenny obviously had no idea what was happening—she thought her mother had passed out from the thrill.

Jefferson could not believe he had lost control in public that way—perhaps it was having both females together in combination with the pretended danger, perhaps it was the proximity of the junk yard—he spent the last half of the ride arousing Carol, helping her get her breath back, apologizing sincerely (although he didn't think she was cognizant of what he was saying), until she was at least able to stagger from the ride with his and Jenny's well-meaning but ineffectual assistance. Several people tittered, obviously thinking she'd had too much beer before the ride. Jefferson relaxed a little—she did, indeed, appear drunk.

He found a place out of view of the crowd, behind some tents at the back of the carnival, where he let her down into soft grass and stretched her out. He gave Jenny a dollar and sent her off for a coke for her mom.

Jefferson slapped Carol's face several times, vaguely excited that he had a good excuse for it, and marveled at the alternating patterns of pallor and redness made when he struck her soft skin.

Suddenly her hand reached up and grabbed his wrist. Her head jerked up and she started choking. "You tried to . . . you tried . . ." Her eyes popped open from the force of her choking, and Jefferson could see the sudden shock of knowledge in them. It seemed as if she had recognized him for the very first time.

"You . . ." she began again, and he threw himself on her, pressing his right shoulder hard into her mouth so that she could not speak and wrapping his arms, his legs around the thrashing, desperate life of her, admiring the energy and will of her, wishing that he had some of that life and will for himself. With alarm, he became aware that he had a growing erection prodding at her lower belly, and anxious to stop this erection he squeezed her head more tightly, he squeezed her neck, needing to consume her before she could consume any part of him.

At last she sighed and rattled and he clamped his mouth over hers to capture this final bit of her breath. And then he heard the soft crying behind him.

He jerked around as Jenny screamed and started through the flimsy wire fence that separated the carnival from the salvage yard. Jefferson rose to go after her but Carol's hand had clutched his left wrist so tightly he could not escape her. He bent over her again and screaming smashed his right fist into her face and arms until at last she released him. He leaped up and ran through the fence, which scratched and clawed him and which he had to kick and smash against until it too would release him. Now he could see Jenny some distance away, running into the valley made between two mountains of ravaged cars, smashed and burned containers for the soft, sickly, all-too-brittle bodies of people.

He quickly closed the gap on the little girl but there were so many twists and turns between the ranks of cars that she was always able to remain just out of his reach. The longer she stayed away from his touch the more he needed to touch her.

Although he pushed himself as hard as he could to catch her, and the vigor of this effort engendered an anger that heightened almost with every step, Jefferson was also rapidly considering how he might prevent himself from killing her. Would it be possible for him to keep her rather than kill her?

If he kept her he could take her out whenever he liked and hug her, squeeze her to his heart's content but of course he'd have to be careful that he didn't do it too often and too hard, perhaps just until she passed out or until she was so afraid she fouled herself or her skin released the toxins preparatory to death. She was a small child, after all, and wouldn't cost that much to feed and surely he could keep such a small child quiet enough for his purposes. Perhaps he could experiment with varying amounts of food and drugs in order to find just the right level to maintain her in a pliable, maximally squeezable, yet still living state.

He rounded the burned-out husk of an ancient DeSoto in time to see Jenny climbing a rust-red mountain of cars directly ahead of him. She was screaming, she had probably been screaming for some time now, but the junkyard was technically closed and the blended screams from the carnival behind him effectively covered all individual sound.

Jefferson leaped to the back of the first car, reached up and grabbed the antique door handle of another and used this to pull himself to the hood of a woody station wagon. Jenny looked back and screamed again, her mouth distorting as if her face were in the process of ripping open and flapping in the breeze. She scrambled over a collapsed Buick and then to the top-most boulder in a pile of stones supporting one side of the stack of cars. Jefferson could see that her knees and shins were badly skinned, bright blood sheeting down as if her small stick-like legs were being peeled. He hoped that she would not injure herself further. Any more damage to her delicate skin and he might not feel so compelled to hold her.

Jenny disappeared from the top of the mountain of cars.

A door panel shifted under Jefferson's foot. A side mirror in his hand broke off and he dropped it to the ground. Glass began to crack softly like ice thawing as more metal moved and slipped and the contours of the rusted mountain underwent a subtle change. He struggled slowly to the summit and looked over. Jenny stared up at him from an empty aisle just beyond the mountain. She turned and ran.

"Jenny!" he screamed, and reached out his hands.

The mountain trembled as the topmost stones which buttressed it slipped from their perch and crashed onto rusted brittle hoods and quarter panels, slamming through partial windshields and changing the perspective of the overlapping vehicles stacked beneath Jefferson's uneasy feet. He looked once again at Jenny's distant running form and thought to hug himself instead as he fell back off the summit and was folded again and again as the mountain unraveled and seven decades worth of cars descended with him.

For a brief sliver of time he thought how he might embrace himself fully, his skin bonding to his own skin and the heart of him becoming so compressed that it was hard and invulnerable to even the strongest touch, and then all the stones and wrecks of time came down upon him and his thought was squeezed to nothing.

SHARP EDGES

In such an intense physical act like murder, between the victim and the murderer there is something sensual... the death orgasm and the sexual one.

—Dario Argento

Jane spent hours shaving her legs, despite the fact that the act tangled her in anxiety. Even in her nervousness, however, the results never failed to fascinate: the warm pink smoothness of the legs, the skin scraped so thin one might have seen the blood pulsing just beneath the surface. Then there were the occasional nicks: in particular the granular abrasions around the heel and ankle, where the skin came so close to the bone it appeared painted on. When first cut open her pale skin pinkened, as if suffused with a new liveliness, then the tiny beads of blood oozed out onto the surface, and Jane found the look and smell of them oddly comforting, like milk for a baby, confirming for her that this life was, indeed, real. Although beneath the surface pleasure, a profound terror lurked.

Jane had many such terrors, and her psychotherapist believed that if she faced the smallest among them first, the grip of her more dramatic fears might begin to loosen. She wasn't sure about this, but would never think of arguing with him. Besides, shaving her legs was important to her appearance.

So when she shaved with the razor she held her breath. It steadied her hand. But there were still the inevitable slips, the skin torn, the pale flesh of the calf washed with a translucent spread of blood. She'd gasp and run to the mirror: staring eyes dilating rapidly in the high polish of the glass. And each time, behind her in the clouds of steam from the shower, she could see the knife blade easing aside the crisp plastic curtain.

Maxwell sawed carefully through the hollow handle of the cane, inserting the narrow knife in one opening and carving out the other end to create a close, smooth-fitting sheath for the blade. He supposed you could purchase such a device, but he felt more comfortable making his own. He doubted his particular version could kill, but killing wasn't what he was after with this instrument. It was intended merely to probe, to produce seemingly accidental scratches, evidence of all the sharp edges a young lady might discover in the standard urban environment.

In the park, conveniently crowded that afternoon, he created a long vertical tear in a young woman's calf as she passed him jogging. Because of her exertions, the shrouding effect of oxygen depletion, he imagined it was several seconds before she felt the pain and by then he was safely around the bend and stepping briskly down another pathway.

In the local supermarket, obscured behind an elaborate tropical fruit display, he was able to spear a much larger woman in her left buttock. He left the store halfway through a long harangue as she threatened the manager and anyone else in view with legal action. Maxwell had been pleased by the symmetry of the blood stain flowering across the back of her dress.

In similar fashion he continued into the evening, poking, prodding, raising the vaguest signature of blood on women of all ages. Although his escape was uncomfortably narrow at times, he felt no real threat to himself during these activities, for he was simply playing the flirtatious tease, the bashful lover. He was seeing who bled and who did not, and how much. Later, much later, and after extensive courtship, he might open their many mouths for a bright red kiss. But such revelations had to be approached slowly. He had always understood that women were shy creatures, reluctant to give up their secrets, which made what they withheld all the more important. Women were men's complement, their supplement, their completion and their explanation. Open up a woman and you might finally know her, and find the missing pieces of yourself.

Maxwell had left his special cane in the car during dinner at Catalina's, a local restaurant sporting an atypical European diner theme, when he saw Jane enter and take a booth a few feet away. As was his habit, he looked to her fingers first, which were a brighter pink near their ends than on the shafts, with very little nail. He assumed she must chew on her fingers to an obsessive degree, and later observations only confirmed this. He would often wonder during their relationship whether her fingers bled much, and if she sucked this blood, and whether she waited for a large amount to well up before licking, or sucked her fingers constantly, taking the blood before it had the opportunity to stain her pale skin.

Although there was nothing particularly dazzling about this young woman in her twenties, she had a pleasant face, long reddish brown hair which was immanently touchable, and people noticed her. He had no immediate explanation for this, but patrons turned their heads when she entered, looked up at her and smiled, and invariably she smiled back, even to the scruffiest of diners. This was dangerous behavior on her part, he concluded after watching these exchanges for several minutes. Obviously people could see that she was the sort of person who would sit down next to a Charles Manson to chat if a Charles Manson were only to smile at her with even vague politeness. She had this pitiable need to please everyone she met. She was soft, vulnerable, a pale Riding Hood in the woods. She was the kind who walked barefoot on a beach strewn with broken glass, not out of bravery or even foolishness really, but simply out of a sense that this is the way one behaves, however wrongheaded her senses might be. Maxwell was immediately drawn to her.

The music in the restaurant was high-pitched, discordant. For some time Jane had intended to eat here—it was only a few blocks from her apartment building. Now she was sorry she'd ever stepped foot in the place, but lacked the will to turn around and leave. What would people think if she did such a thing? People smiled at her, their eyes reddened by the harsh, crimson neon that was a major component of the decor, neon in primary greens and blues casting mutant shadows around their hunched forms. Some colors might have been surgically removed from the spectrum here: yellow, orange, other tones she couldn't quite put her finger on, making flesh tones darker than they should be, shadows deeper, the air thicker. The acoustics in the restaurant could not have been more harsh. A loud, screaming song under laid with raspy, asthmatic whispering filled her head. She kept smiling, as if to distract her face's need to wince from the pain.

She sat where the blank-faced host directed her, only his teeth gleaming in his dark blue and green face. He led her through a series of patios, past several sets of sliding doors with knifelike edges. Her silverware looked wrong, as if designed for a slightly different species of human being. She sorted through the silverware looking for familiar instruments as the music rose to a bleeding screech in the background.

Bright red and green clouds of light descended around the table. Softer whispers swarmed out of the night, drawn into the bright colors. A man in a dapper dark suit rose at a table a few feet away and began making his way toward her. Nearing her, he looked down and smiled. He leaned over. And stole the knife from beside her plate, slipping it into his coat pocket. She was too shocked and embarrassed to say anything. He grinned a sharp-toothed grin and leaned closer. She imagined she could smell the blood welling to the surface of his warm, pink tongue. He clicked his teeth as if he was going to bite her. Her teeth sawed on the inner surface of her lower lip. His tongue was like a snake's. Her face suffused with heat so quickly she thought she might faint. She closed her eyes. And felt the caress of a blade gliding up her upper arm and slipping just under the edge of her short sleeve, pausing there to tease before turning and gliding out again. She did not realize he had cut her until the sharp stinging began that snatched her breath away. When she opened her eyes again, the man was gone.

In the car Maxwell fingered the edge of the table knife. A session with the whetstone would make it much keener. He brought it up to his nose and sniffed: the rusty bouquet of blood, mingled with perfume reminiscent of lilacs, and a heady, day-old sweat. This was his first gift from her, but he knew there would be many others. And he had many gifts for her as well. She was so naive, so... uninformed. She did not know, yet, that human bodies were thin-walled, fragile, prone to leaks, vulnerable to even the mildest prick from earrings, the rough edge of a necklace, the awkward slip of a comb. A few cuts across the eyeballs would make her see the things she always ignored.

He waited until she left the restaurant, then followed her to her building. The angular trees outside the entrance provided him with cover while he observed which of the mailboxes just inside the door she opened for her mail. A quick peek at the box after she'd gone upstairs, and he knew her exact name and address.

Jane worked as an entry-level secretary in a large corporate law office downtown. It was a job which did little to alter her basic anxiety at being in the world. People were so demanding there, so difficult to satisfy. Every day she felt like more of a failure, less able to please the people she worked for and the people she worked with. She didn't understand what they wanted from her. She didn't know what she had to do to get them to like her.

She might have enjoyed her job more if it hadn't been for all the paper cuts she kept getting, criss-crossing her fingertips in delicate, almost beautiful patterns. Their number increased with her fatigue, certainly, but there were days in which sharp edges seemed intent on her, lying in wait on tabletops, in letter trays, and in her desk drawers.

"Jane! Watch out!"

Jane screamed once in shock and pain. The dangling earring on her left side had caught in the file drawer, pulled through the hole, ripped through the ear. The file room went dark, highlighted in shades of red.

Someone had put a pillow under her head. The whispers of her co-workers grew harsh and garbled above her. They seemed to rise and fall in volume with her pain, eventually blending into an overwhelming, physically-based melody.

A man in a bright blue coat crouched over her. His smile was too broad and thin to be natural. She was embarrassed to have him see her like this. She worried about her dress, her hair. He held up a syringe as if measuring it with his eyes.

As if on its own, the needle reached out and pricked her.

The needle was so thin it became invisible as it entered her flesh. If all edges were so very sharp, perhaps she wouldn't have minded. She wondered with the pleasant vagueness of dream if sunlight had such a super normally sharp edge, if, in fact, it stabbed you to release your darker colors.

She fantasized asking one of her friends in the office to drive her home, but then realized she didn't have any friends.

At home she lay back into her pillows and stared out the window which pressed against the side of her bed. Her ear was covered by a small oval bandage like a cap. These clear glass panes were her only safe windows to the world. And yet, if they were to break she'd surely slash her throat on their edges.

Altogether the room felt less safe than at any time she could remember. Shadows in the room seemed somehow keener than they should have been, even when cast by soft, rounded objects such as pillows and bed corners. She dozed off and on, and every time she opened her eyes the room felt sharper-edged. The surfaces of the pillows were dusty, grittier with each new awakening. She turned her head: angular edges of ceiling littered their primary-colored cases. She glanced up: cracks in the ceiling, edges peeling, falling.

A hard, rhythmic scraping was working its way through the bed and into successive layers of her skin. She glanced down at her hands: her fingers frustrated, attempting to rip the sheets with her chewed-away nails.

The sudden screech of the doorbell cut through the thick bedroom air. She staggered into her robe and down the stairs. Her ear felt wet, as if it had started bleeding again, but when she raised her hand to the stiff bandage her fingers came away dry.

She became acutely aware of small details as she passed through her apartment: the triangular pattern on the dishes, the swirling topography left by the vacuum in the rug, the colored bits in a Teddy Bear's glass eye. After a long day away she focused on such things with every return trip to her apartment, but this afternoon they seemed to be demanding increased attention.

On the other side of the door was a man in a cap, a bundle in his arms. The peephole brought her a reassuring slice of him: bland, sunshiny, smiling face, a florist's symbol on the cap, a bundle of flowers in his hand. She opened the door a minimal amount. "Miss Jane Akers?" She nodded; she took the flowers.

It was after she closed the door firmly behind her that she felt the pricking around the stems, and discovered that sharp wire bound the flower arrangement together, short sections of it twisted together as on a barbed-wire fence. Her fingers grew sticky where they'd been punctured; juice from the stems made them sting. There was no card.

She thought she heard a throaty whispering in the apartment which disappeared every time she tried to focus on it. But for several weeks there had been a continuous thread of barely-detectable whispering, murmured beneath taped music, within the background static of phone conversations, between the lines of television commercials, so to hear it today, after so much trauma, should not have been surprising.

She didn't want the flowers—she despised them. But she couldn't just throw them in the trash. You weren't supposed to throw flowers away; you were supposed to put them in water. So she did. She wondered if the barbed wire would rust. Feeling she could not stay here another minute, she got on her coat and opened the door, intent on walking out of her anxiety.

Maxwell watched the florist's van pull away from the front of her apartment building. It had been easy enough to find a young man eager to make the extra money, without asking embarrassing questions. Maxwell had stood by the outside door and witnessed the entire transaction, and had been touched by the way she'd pulled the flowers into her arms so desperately, as if starved for affection. It made him love her even more.

She was shy, yet eager for love—he could sense this about her. She was his discovery. He was sure he could make contact with a woman like this—he was convinced she was reachable, unlike so many other women who frightened him. He could make contact—if not with his heart, then with his knife.

Now she was leaving the building, walking briskly down the street, her chin pushed forward as if in defiance. He smiled and checked the Polaroid camera on the seat beside him, the extra film cartridges in the box beside it. He started the car.

Jane had no particular destination in mind, but she would know where she was going when she got there. She stared at the far away trees, the gray outlines of buildings reaching into the dark city mists. On the face of a distant tower, giant clock hands sliced through the misty air, releasing its toll like a damp explosion.

She passed a black metal fence, its vertical bars spinning by her like film frames. The sharp points along the top of the wrought iron leaned in her direction, aiming at her soft flesh.

People lounged along the edges of the sidewalk and on the grassy verge of the park spreading out in front of her. Were they waiting for her? Their noses showed the sharp profile of cartilage. Their jaws were blades, their chins the points. They stared at her with their thin, sharp smiles. She wanted to say something that would make them like her, but she didn't know the right words.

A lizard crawled out of the grass directly in front of her, as if to divert her attention. She thought of stepping on its back, shuddered, and moved away from it.

At the north gate of the park a man had set up a table and was selling brushes and combs. A succession of combs lined a tray covered with black velvet. He grinned at her as he brushed his fingers across their fine teeth. "A lovely comb for the lovely lady?"

He scared her, but it would be rude to hurry past. "They're so pretty," she said, looking down at the pitiful selection. "How much is that one?" she asked, pointing to the cleanest looking one.

"For you, a buck."

She gave him a dollar at the end of trembling fingers. He touched the dollar, but then his whole hand moved up to clutch her arm. "Such a pretty girl."

She smiled nervously, on the verge of tears. She wanted to scream, but what if he was really nice? He bent down and kissed her fingers with lips that felt slick and oily. "Have a nice day," he said, letting go of her arm and handing her the comb. She made herself smile again, then walked away, rubbing the back of her hand on her coat, trying to wipe away the feel of his lips.

She approached a row of storefronts. Soft explosions of brilliant light occurred behind her, but when she turned around there was nothing there. She looked up at the sky: dark clouds were piling one atop the other, their edges rubbed shiny where lightning had gathered.

She looked into the window of a hardware store: an axe, shovel, shears. Then several clothing boutiques: black gloves, black lace. Sexless beings dressed completely in black: hats, gloves, black leather coats.

She imagined she could hear the sounds of zippers snagging flesh from deep inside these shops, the customers weeping softly.

She was vaguely aware of someone taking photos of her, but when she turned around no one was there.

She had to step over an old man in dark glasses, lying with his german shepherd, both of them sprawled across the middle of the sidewalk. The old man's cane came up, pointing at her like an arrow. The dog turned and bared its teeth, then lunged for the pasty flesh of the man's wrinkled hand. The man yelled. Blood sprayed in a mist across the sidewalk.

She looked past the wounded man at another man standing in a doorway. His damp lips and glistening eyes, watching her. His hands clutching, as if they held the stolen table knife. But she knew this wasn't the same man.

Thunder crashed behind her. For a second the city skyline appeared to be on fire, a giant camera scorching it as picture after picture was taken. Rain began, then suddenly became a downpour.

Even through the heavy rain she could see them all staring at her. Jane found sanctuary beneath a large store awning. On the other side of the glass, an elderly woman was cutting shapes out of black paper, demonstrating silhouette portraiture. Jane thought she recognized the profile the old woman was working on as her own.

The woman looked up, gasping as she peered into Jane's face. The scissors slipped and cut through the face of the silhouette.

Jane ran back out into the rain. Music crashed inside her head. The storm sounded like the same music. She gazed past the gray buildings, searching, intent on returning to her apartment. The rain slackened some. She entered the park. Blades of leaves, blades of grass. Children had gathered by the north gate and were playing with a lizard. There was no sign of the man selling combs. Another bright, soft explosion, but Jane didn't bother to look up this time. She gazed more closely at the children. Their lizard wriggled madly, nailed through its neck to a board. She suddenly burned hot with shame.

The centerpiece of the park was an arrangement of giant metal sculptures with razor-thin planes, broad fields of metal. At first glance the sculptures appeared curvilinear, but closer examination revealed hidden points, sharp edges residing within the folds of illusory soft steel and brass.

She ran past the sculptures as another bright flash almost blinded her, and suddenly a pigeon was flapping at her side, caught on the huge button of her coat sleeve. Its claws came out and dug a ridge into the flesh covering the back of her hand.

She finally shook the bird loose, crying loudly as it pecked her. No one came to her aid. The world was full of too many sharp edges. It was pointless to get too deeply involved. You risked your own death. She ran the few remaining blocks, the rain beating the blood away as it struggled to escape her cuts.

She slammed the apartment door behind her. Someone had dropped a shiny, brightly-colored magazine through her mail slot. She picked it up. Inside, nude photos of women had been scored horizontally repeatedly with a razorblade, turning their flesh into venetian blinds.

Maxwell used up all his film, and he would have loved to have had several more packs. The passion in her face as she ran away from the man with the cane, the trapped bird—he would have given anything to have had such passion directed at him. He loved her more with each stolen glimpse of intense emotion. He hoped the magazine he had left for her demonstrated just how much she made him feel, how badly he wanted to reach her, make contact, and banish his loneliness forever.

When Jane threw the magazine to the floor a note fell from its pages. She ripped the envelope open frantically, jerking the folded letter out with shaking fingers. His handwriting consisted of thin, jagged uprights, virtually unreadable. Love . . . sharp . . . you . . . reach: these were the only words she could make out.

A crashing in the alley. Garbage can lids banged out a crazed musical. She crept to the back door that led to the fire escape and pulled it open. The alley was silent, empty.

She closed the door and turned back into the hallway which ran the length of her apartment. She stepped on something soft and pliant. She reached down and picked up the worn leather glove. A man's glove: who was responsible for it? It was stained here and there a dark color, a shade of red like ancient rust.

Bright neon from the hotel sign outside the window at the end of the hall washed the walls a more brilliant red. The tall curtains on either side of the window swept the floor, gliding in and out as if the window were a mouth, breathing. She knew there were sharp blades behind the billowing curtains, an erect penis behind the soft gabardine swaddling the crotch of the man who might be hiding there.

She could not stay here any longer. In her makeup mirror she paid particular attention to the jagged patterns in her eyes, but no cosmetic could smooth these. It was all a part of being in the world, she supposed, but now she did not know if she wanted to be a part of the world or not. She glanced at her clock: impossibly, it said she had been back in her apartment for hours.

She finally gave up on returning a semblance of normalcy

to her face, put on her coat again, and left her apartment to go see a movie. At least she could be assured that in the movie theatre, nothing is real.

Maxwell wondered if Jane had read his note yet, if she had glanced through his magazine, if she had discovered his intentionally dropped glove. Simple things, but they had the power to agitate the imagination of those vulnerable enough to suggestion. The innocent knew that the world was a dangerous place, but they were incapable of fully appreciating the implications.

In the two hours since he had left Jane's apartment, he had been quite busy. The close proximity of her things had aroused him, so he immediately went out looking for a substitute for her.

The woman hadn't wanted to return home with him, but it never ceased to amaze him how easily obstacles could be gotten rid of by means of a simple act of murder.

He enjoyed dancing. It was the only time he could hold a live woman with safety. But death made this one an even better dancing partner than he was used to. He had to tie her body to his waist and legs, but once this had been accomplished she followed him perfectly, now and then rolling her head onto his shoulder in affection. A pity he was already taken.

He hadn't caught her name before, but he preferred making up his own names anyway. "Janice," for this one, as she was to be Jane's substitute for the moment. With the wound in her face, Janice was completely possessable: a marred masterpiece, a "second" available for a reduced price, reduced effort. But she remained a great work of art for all that.

As the music rose to a crescendo, he recalled the moments of Janice's creation: how he had heard her heart in his head, beating, struggling to escape the point of his knife (but not Jane's knife—he would never betray Jane in that fashion), how again and again he had thrust the point into the center of her beating, until the sound had faded from his head.

She had struggled, but all too briefly. She had kicked a bit;

as if in a dream he had felt her high heels puncturing his flesh, marking him in subtle and not-so-subtle ways.

Now the dance was over. The music ran down. Maxwell grasped the knife handle still protruding from Janice's chest. He pulled down on the knife. Her flesh split like rotted silk. He gasped with pleasure as the blade sliced through blouse, slip, skin.

He gasped again and again, louder than the music screaming in his head.

As she walked to the movie, the passersby whispered among themselves, too loudly for comfort, in fact far more loudly than was possible.

She might have gone to the police, but what could she tell them? She'd received a garbled note, a damaged magazine, and someone had lost a glove, someone had stolen a knife from a local restaurant. Her co-workers would be questioned, and they would talk about how nervous "Poor Jane" had always been, how high-strung, how no one in the office really liked her. She would be embarrassed in front of the police; they would be disappointed in her.

She put on her glasses before entering the movie, intending to wear them for the rest of the night. She'd always felt protected behind the thick lenses. Even when she witnessed something terrible—a workman's hand slashed open on a dagger of glass, a young boy stabbed just above the groin in a schoolyard fight—she felt shielded by that thickness from the full weight of these incidents. They could not touch her on the other side of the glass. The images would not adhere to the filmy surface of her eyes.

But there was also this accompanying sense of danger: glass that so shielded her might break if the images came too close.

The theatre darkened; the previews came up with amplified color and volume. What little light remained reflected off all the sharp edges hidden in the theatre. A few minutes into the movie she realized she had seen it before, but she knew she wouldn't be watching the screen anyway. Instead, she gazed at the backs of people's heads, the placement of their arms on companions' shoulders, their small open displays of affection, and observed how they reacted to the murders taking place on the screen.

Maxwell had always enjoyed the company of mannequins. So intent on looking a certain way for their male customers, they did not speak back. He envied their makers.

He bundled Janice, the mannequin he had created, into a bag and brought her back to Jane's apartment during the movie—he had passed Jane on the way over, and followed her until he was sure of her destination. If he worked quickly, he knew he could be outside the movie theatre when the film ended.

The lock on the apartment door had jimmied easily. Poor, naive Jane. Her lack of informed caution filled him with a renewed tenderness toward her. On the bed, blood dripped down the mannequin's arm, paused in the openness of the relaxed palm, then leapt from the forefinger to the carpet below.

He took the Polaroids he had made of Jane and spread them carefully across her dining room table. He laid one against the other, matching patterns, shadows, stances, expressions. He permitted one image of her to kiss another image of her. His fingers lingered over her glossy surfaces. He meditated on the silkiness of her image. He took a pair of scissors from the drawer and laid one blade across a photograph, bisecting her face. He moved the blades together until her head disappeared. He raised one of the photographs, poised the twin points of the scissors over the image of her breasts, and pierced them simultaneously with one quick jab. He then began cutting through each of the photographs, disassembling each image of her until he had a large pile of shiny pieces. A bottle of bright red nail polish, retrieved from her vanity, sat poised on the edge of her fragmented poses. He took this and began painting the pile of clippings with red swirls, arrows, and bright red hearts.

He picked up a meat cleaver from her kitchen counter and used it to dismember the graceful lines of the bed stead, the side table, the dresser. He slashed through the bed clothes and started on the contents of her closet. He arranged the mannequin within the destroyed womb of her bed, then began hacking on it as well, imprinting it with all his secret signatures. Then, seeing himself in the mirror of the vanity, the glittering blade in his upraised hand, he started smashing his own image in the mirror.

Jane felt a heightened self-consciousness leaving the movie theatre. She thought they must see her awkwardness, the wrongness in her. The crowd seemed subdued, as was often the case when people departed this sort of entertainment, as they attempted to extricate their thoughts and eyes from the webs and tendrils of fantasy. She felt as if she herself were too well-defined today, her terror too palpable against the crowd's backdrop of oh-so-gray emotion. It made her too-involved, vulnerable, an easy target.

A dark murmuring in the crowd off to her left, but Jane was determined not to look. She and the others around her crunched through powdered glass on the sidewalk, no doubt the remains of some wino's refreshment.

Soon she was at the edge of the park, an unusually bright streetlight mounted on the entrance above her. The sharp edges of light dropped painfully through the narrow, dark tree branches. In the distance, she could see women running away from the park. Beyond the sharp sculptures, Jane thought she could hear women screaming in windows.

He saw her stumbling through the park toward him, drawn along like a fly on the web of his personality, her face contorted as if from some massive, internal noise. He enjoyed the feel of insects blown against his skin, scratching across his arms and face, dancing. He withdrew the table knife from his pocket, its blade sharpened to a thin blue edge. He stroked it slowly, ready to make contact, ready to make love to her.

Jane saw him standing in front of the sculptures, their metal edges surrounded by clouds of dark insects as they attempted to tear holes in the sky. People were fleeing the park. Why was she just standing there? It was the dapper older man from the restaurant, the one who had stolen her table knife, the one who had been pursuing her. She wondered if perhaps a kiss, or even just a hug, might satisfy him and make him leave her alone.

His teeth gleamed. She turned and ran. Away from her apartment, away from the park, and as he pursued her, running ahead of her here, heading her off there, she realized she could only go where he wanted her to go.

She ran down an alley with the man pacing steadily behind her. She barked her left knee against a torn metal drum; dampness spread rapidly down her leg. Cats scattered madly as she escaped the alley, as she crossed one street and then another, as she entered a shattered block of buildings, all condemned for the cinema complex to be erected there soon, a third of the buildings already gnawed into submission by the parked machinery.

She made her way through the jumbles of debris which filled the ruins, tormented by wood splinters and insect bites. Nails protruded from raw wounds in the wood, anxious to match their scars with her own.

She stopped, staring into the night in front of her. Suddenly his eyes peered from two holes carved out of the darkness. She spun right and broke through a flimsy door, into a building with dim yellow lights in its cracked windows, the only such lighting on the block.

Mannequins littered the hallway. Pieces of clothing hung

from scattered plastic arms and heads. A battered hat. A leather glove. A red rain coat. A stocking mask.

She ran through an open door, into a bedroom. Several lamps affixed with colored bulbs burned before a mirror on the large dressing table. A cat moved listlessly across piles of broken plaster toward her. It seemed to have unusually short hair; then she realized it had been shaved down to tissue-thin skin. Under the colored lights, the shaved cat's skin looked blood-red. She leaned over and stroked it—it was too drugged to purr. She could see veins laboring just under the surface of the skin. A diagram had been drawn in black permanent marker under its torso, like a butcher's chart.

Four naked cats lay near the dusty red bed (a bed for lovers, she thought), their tiny throats cut.

And then she heard him out in the hallway, whispering his love for her.

She crashed through the next door into an old kitchen with its piles of rusted silverware and broken plates and cups—smeared with dark, blood-like stains—littering the gray linoleum floor. Her feet, now bare, scraped across the shattered edges. The walls echoed complexly. She imagined them riddled with secret doors and passages, but more likely it was the effects of generations of rot.

She passed through another door into a hall a bit more barren than the first. Most of the ceiling bulbs in the hall were broken, their curved jigsaw pieces breaking under her bare feet like deadly eggshells, barbed edges gleaming under the remaining yellow light.

A loud noise behind her and she fell into agony. She scrambled up and stared at her left arm: a sharp shaft of bone jutted from her broken skin.

She leapt back across the hall and slammed the door into the kitchen, painfully turning the old-fashioned latch. A knife blade suddenly appeared in the crack between the door and the jamb, working its way down toward the latch. The man laughed softly, whispering love songs as he worked.

She jerked her head around, searching for the next escape. A staircase led downward. She hobbled over and stumbled down the steps.

Animal teeth scattered on the floor, rats in the corners, nesting. A Polaroid of a sliced eyeball had been nailed to the wall beneath a precisely mounted spotlight. Below this was the body it had been taken from: she thought she recognized him as the man who had sold her a comb earlier that day.

Another body lay at the end of the short, subterranean hallway: maggots had blunted the sharp planes of the face and made a curlicue border along the dark hair line, but it still bore a startling resemblance to a woman who used to sell tickets at the movie theatre.

In a small, clean room she found another woman's body, razor blades embedded in cheeks and neck tendons. A scratching at the small window near the ceiling made her turn her head. The glass broke, as if in slow motion, across her face. It showered down before her like frozen, glittering, magical tears.

First arms, then a head, burst through the rainbow-sheened glass. The man from the restaurant grinned at her through the blood washing over his face. He looked down at the cement floor, where he had dropped his knife.

She stooped and picked up the knife off the floor. She stroked its smooth handle. She imagined using it, slipping it through clothing into flesh and beyond. She imagined making love to the man's body with it, kissing him all over with it, until he cried. It made her feel strange, imagining a man's tears, imagining a man's submission.

Maxwell stared at his lover through a dull red filter. Her constant screams of passion had receded as they blended with the loud music in his head, until eventually he could not distinguish the two melodies. He desperately wanted her to join him with the knife, to make of them one creature, to blend their blood streams until they were, finally, one single, gaping wound.

But then he found himself falling the rest of the way through the basement window, glass and blood descending with him as he flew away to regions of dream.

Only when her voice finally gave out into a raw, bleeding whisper did she realize she had been screaming constantly since her discovery of the first body. The scream joined the frantic music which still filled her head.

She struck out against him even as he crashed into her, but in the course of their struggles dropped the knife. She was surprised to find him naked but for his bright red uniform of blood—at some point he had stripped away all pretension. His toenails felt like metal against her body, but his fingernails were so sharp she did not feel them at all when they slid beneath the surface of her skin.

He brought the edge of his hand down on her cheekbone, filling her vision with bright, blinding flashes of light. He grinned at her, and dipped his finger into the blood covering his face, and drew a bright red line across her neck.

She rose onto her knees and rolled, and he rolled with her, his teeth biting her ear as he whispered her name. They crashed into the door, closing it firmly on the hall and the little light it had provided.

A glint in the dark, a flat surface catching any available light. His hand was on it, and raising it high above her head.

The knife passed through her hand, nailing it to the door. She spat into his face and he pulled the knife out and thrust it at her again. The point passed through the surface of her right cheek. She stretched out her arms to ward off the blows: the blade bit at the fleshy areas of her palms, her fingers, releasing exclamations of blood. She jerked forward, catching him off-guard, jamming the webbing of her damaged hand into his throat. He fell back and she was on her feet again, slamming open the door and running back into the hall. She turned and scrambled up a pile of crates to a screened window, her hands leaving red prints on everything she touched.

Then he was behind her, pushing her face roughly into the large squares of wire mesh. She could feel the checkerboard pattern etching into her soft skin. Getting her feet beneath her, she pushed back against a crate launching them both backward through the air. She could feel something breaking beneath her, something in the man's body, as they slammed into the floor. But he simply groaned and said, "Darling."

Across the hall there was the open door to a dingy bathroom. She crawled up off the man and scrambled through the door on her hands and knees, locking it behind her. She stood up. The bathroom was brightly lit by six huge incandescent bulbs mounted in the ceiling. Judging from the heat they gave off, she imagined they had been burning for some time. Blood like red greasepaint smeared the fixtures. On the other side of the door a high-pitched man's voice—imitating a woman—began chanting her name.

She screamed back at him, "What did I do? I'm a nice person!" Then she laughed huskily, the laughter bringing bile up her raw throat.

A knife blade slipped through a crack in the door panel, moving back and forth first in a sawing motion, then a chiseling one. She grabbed a piece of broken pipe off the floor and started swinging at the blade, finally snapping it off. She released a strained whoop of victory. "What kind of lover would you be?" she screamed through the door.

"I loved you!" the man shouted on the other side.

Jane collapsed into bleating laughter. The loud music faded from her head, exhausting her. "No one can make love to me," she said, finally, quietly. "I am too afraid of all these sharp edges."

A thundering on the other side of the door, and then the door disintegrated in rage around her. Clouds of dust floated in brilliant crimson light.

• • •

Maxwell saw himself in the bathroom's mirrored, blood-stained wall. Jane's face floated at his knees, gazing up at his reflection in a way which resembled longing, but which he knew might be any emotion at all. He realized, now, that he could never know what Jane really felt about anything. With a scream he plunged the blade into his own belly. He looked down at what he had done to himself, examining the knife handle curiously, as if it were his umbilical cord suddenly reappeared after all these years.

He sank to his knees behind her, touching her torn shoulder with one hand.

"I am too afraid," she said.

"We're all afraid," he said.

"Am I going to die now?" she asked.

"No," he replied, gazing down at the blood seeping from his belly. She did not move away. He would always be thankful for that, as he closed his eyes, and in his long dream carried her back upstairs and into his bed.

WET KISSES IN THE DARK

I let myself in with the key she had given me and tried the light switch by the door. Nothing. I stepped into the living room, outlined in the yellow neon that seeped through the windows from the fast food place across the street. Paper crinkled under my shoes and there was a sharp crunch now and then like she'd left cracker crumbs or bits of pretzel all over the floor. And sharp smells like cheese and liquor and bad perfume, but then Liz had always been a lousy housekeeper. I could never have lived with her, myself.

I tried the light switch by the dining room. Still nothing. Now I figured it was a fuse problem. The whole circuit was out.

The rhythmic shush of the cars out on the wet pavement was so loud they sounded like they were in the next room. The fractured reflections of their headlights washed the dining room walls in waves. Dark patches spotted the walls. Even with that stingy bit of light, I could see that bowls of food had been turned upside down on the table.

Somewhere in the apartment there was a snuffling sound, then a wet whimper. "Liz?" I moved toward the bedroom.

She was sitting on the floor, down in the shadows by the bed. "You're a little late..." she said softly, with the hint of a slur. I figured she'd started drinking when I didn't show up on time. I really couldn't complain, however; I'd had five or six gin and tonics and a couple of beers myself before coming over. They'd filled up the spaces, and these days I felt like I had a lot of spaces.

"Honey, I'm sorry. It was hard to get away."

"It's always hard to get away. So what? You still gotta do it."

"You've been drinking."

She laughed. "I've never been more sober. Come sit beside me, lover."

So I went over and I sat down. The carpet there was damp. In the dim light I couldn't see her expression, just a white sliver of teeth, the blue cast in one of her eyes. "So why the dark? You didn't pay your bill?"

She laughed again. "That's just like you, lover. Everybody knows it's more romantic in the dark."

"I don't know from romance, but I like to see what it is I'm getting into."

She laughed again, leaned over, and gave me a big, sloppy kiss. Her lips were wet and salty, like those pretzels maybe, and smeared with something sweet and heavy. A sauce or a chili, I couldn't tell; the liquor had killed my taste buds. Then I thought about the spilled food in the dining room. "What's all the mess out there? I take it Walter didn't like dinner again? That why you invited me over?"

She chuckled wetly. "Walter never liked my cooking. We had a fight, that's all. Now come here and taste some more of me. That's what you came for, isn't it? Not to criticize my housekeeping."

She had a point. I edged closer, then stopped. Something about the way she smelled. "How long you been sitting here? You hurt or something?"

Liz laughed so hard she started coughing, coughing so hard I thought she was going to choke on it. "No, lover. Way past hurt."

I felt awkward sitting there beside her, especially with the funny way she smelled, so I got up and sat on the edge of her bed. Their bed. Walter's and hers. "So is he coming back any-time soon? You guys have a big fight?"

She snorted. "And you're horny, right? You want to get something going before he gets back? Well, get back down here on the floor. I don't want to mess up the bed."

I was mad, and I was getting disgusted. I didn't like being around Liz when she was drunk. And the way she smelled—I was beginning to think that maybe'd she'd wet herself. "I was just showing my concern, Liz. If you weren't such a mess you'd see that. Christ… at least you could straighten things up around here. What'd you two do, have a food fight or something?"

"Is that what you tell your wife? You tell her she should be cleaning the house better? Is that your excuse for going out and finding something on the side? Something like me?"

I held my breath, thinking fast, but having no real place to go, the thinking just running around in circles. So I stopped thinking. "How'd you find out?"

"Walter told me all about it. He explained things real good."

"So Walter found out about us? Or did you just go and tell him? Dammit, Liz."

"Walter wasn't stupid. Not like me. I guess he knew for a long time. He said you were just playing with me. He laughed a lot when he told me that. I always used to hate it when Walter laughed at me like that. Like I was the dumbest person he'd ever heard of. And maybe I was."

Right then I knew I was supposed to correct her. No, hon. You're one smart lady, you are. Don't let him put you down. He just doesn't understand you. That had always been my role. But I just couldn't do it. Maybe it was because she smelled so bad. How could you tell a woman she was smart when there was crap all over the walls and the floor and she smelled so bad? "You better get yourself cleaned up." It was all I could think of to say. "Maybe I can help you." I prayed she'd say no. I was trying to figure out a good exit line. I wasn't liking being alone in the dark with her, even though before that night I'd wanted it all the time. You and me in the dark, hon. And then she'd be kissing me all over, her lips wet, her teeth scraping just enough to excite me. Wet kisses in the dark. She'd been so good at that. Who cared that she was a lousy housekeeper? I wasn't her husband.

"I can't get clean. Not this time. No, not going to work this time."

"C'mon, Liz. How much you have to drink, anyway? He'll be back. Probably bring you some candy and roses. Walter's got no spine. You told me that yourself."

She started laughing again, and I just wanted to leave. I couldn't stand being in that room. I thought I was going to be sick. "No, not this time, lover," she said. "You're lying about that one. And you were always so good at lying. Guess you're losing your touch." She clamped her lips over my mouth then, and stuck that thick, salty tongue of hers inside me, and then I was so full of the sad smell of her I couldn't breathe anymore. I started to choke and I pushed her away. My hands came away from her shoulders warm and sticky.

"Christ! What is this stuff? You throw up on yourself, Liz? Jesus! It's like you've been swimming in garbage!"

"Oh, I have, lover. You and me . . . pure garbage. Walter knew that, too. My Walter wasn't such a dumb man after all. He knew garbage when he smelled it. That's more than I can say for you, lover."

"I don't need this crap."

"Oh? You get this 'crap' at home, lover? Is that why you're with me three nights a week? Not enough crap at home?"

"I'm outta here." I pushed myself off the damp carpet and leaned onto the edge of the bed. That's when she grabbed my ankle and twisted, trying to pull me back down. I jerked myself away from her and sprawled across the bed. On top of somebody else.

A hand caught in the lining of my coat. Trying to unsnag myself I rolled over a face. The lips were wet, smearing across me. The chest was wet. Liquid had pooled in the hollow of the belly.

"Whaaa . . .!"

Liz's damp chuckle stopped me before I could get all the way off the bed. Then she had her hands around my ankles again. "You like threesomes, lover? Walter's not gonna mind."

I cried out and tried to kick her but it only made me lose my balance. Before I knew it the dark came up and slammed me in the face. The fuse blew. And I was out.

I don't know how long I was unconscious. Probably not all that long, but long enough for Liz to crawl up on top of me, pinning me to the floor. She was a small woman, but right then she felt like she weighed three hundred pounds. Her clothes were soggy, heavy against my skin. She'd gotten my coat off. And my shirt. My pants were unzipped and something cold, something metal, was rubbing up against me down there.

"Liz..." I knew it came out like a hiss, like I was all excited. It scared me, that was all. I couldn't help it.

"Make love to me, lover. That's what you do. Love me, now. Garbage against garbage."

"Liz." I sucked air. She'd jabbed the cold metal hard into me.

She laughed, then she moaned, like the noises I was making excited her. But I couldn't help it. "Shut up and kiss me," she said, and her wet lips moved across my face and found my mouth, and then I recognized that taste. Maybe I'd recognized that taste all along and just couldn't admit it. That warm, salty, metal taste. That coppery smell.

I turned my head away. "No."

She slapped me across the face and jabbed harder with the cool steel. Something thick dripped off her head onto my nose, into my eyes. She bent down and she kissed me. She forced my lips open with her teeth and she bit them. "Walter likes to watch," she said. "We're going to let him watch now. Usually he does it from the closet, in the dark. He told me all about it. We had no idea; Walter's not so dumb. But watching us from the bed is better. That way he won't miss anything."

"Liz..." My throat hurt; she'd clogged it with her own blood. "I cared about you."

"Liar!" She tried to scream it but she couldn't. "Walter told me all about it while he was using the knife on me, the one that was lying by the roast beef just waiting for him. I always tried to get him dinner on time. He told me how he'd watched you with your wife and kids, how happy you looked, how you kissed her every morning. The way she smiled. Walter knew all about men, he told me all about men. How they're always looking for something on the side. And how it isn't personal. How it isn't personal at all."

"Liz, please…" I started to choke. Then I started to cry.

"Please yourself, lover. Make love to me. Make love to me with my husband watching us. Make it good because it's the last time. Walter saw to that. He's hurt me bad."

She jabbed the gun into my groin. "Oh, Jesus, don't hurt me!"

"I'm not going to hurt you, just slip out of these pants. I'll help you, if you help me. Take your pants off." Wiggling, squirming in panic, I did. "Good. Good. I won't hurt you. Just make love to me and I won't hurt you. I won't shoot you. I promise. You'll have a good time. Make love to me while Walter watches from the bed. I'm dying, lover. I'm dying hard. Make love to me hard. Do it right and all the time you won't be able to tell if I'm still alive, or if I'm dead yet. You won't be able to tell."

She was right. I couldn't.

THE STENCH

It is the smell of the body laboring for survival. It is the stink of fear. It is the odor of cooking and cleaning and the lingering aroma of sex in darkened rooms. It is the reek of poverty and the sharp tang of desperation. It is the sour bouquet of bodies aging into death, the whiff of illness and the fragrance of failing organs. It is the scent and the sense of sadness that comes with realizations hard won. It is the stench.

Riley had no use for uncleanliness. He'd been raised by grandparents who by the end of their lives had lost their sense of smell. They did not know how unpleasant the odors from their bodies had become, although he thought his grandmother sometimes guessed, judging by her periodic and frantic binges of scrubbing and scouring on hands and knees as if praying before some ferocious god. But these spells would pass and when next he was in her proximity his nose would hum and his eyes water from the smell of her dying in the small rooms of their farmhouse.

His grandfather claimed that food had turned on him years back, barely able to nourish him and unpleasant in both taste and digestion. He'd spent long hours each day locked in the bathroom, and walking around the house smelled like a leaky oil furnace ready to explode.

Riley had left his grandparents at a relatively young age, unwilling to wait with them to some inevitable and unpleasant conclusion. He'd felt compelled to travel to the city in order to secure employment, even though it was the most unsanitary place he could imagine. Here you were forced to walk closely with other people, breathing the air directly from their mouths, rubbing against their sweat and touching what tens of thousands had touched before. Whenever possible he bundled up well, covering as much skin as he could, wearing gloves when he thought he could without drawing too much attention. For the last thing he wanted to do was to draw attention to himself.

"A quarter, please, sir? All I need is a quarter."

At first he couldn't find the source of the request and wondered if he'd imagined it or caught a stray fragment of conversation from some passing car. Then he saw the rag-wrapped figure, so close to him he should have not only seen but smelled it.

A woman. There were no obvious signs of femininity, only a patch of unwashed face peering from the rags, but somehow unmistakably a woman. "What was that?" He was too off-balance to think of stepping away.

"A quarter, a dime, whatever you can spare?" A rank scum on corn-colored teeth. Riley could not imagine what she could have eaten to create such a stench. Her eyes were lightly shielded by the worn cloth covering her head. Riley thought of untouchables, lepers, blind beggars in some Asian slum.

"You'll just... you'll just drink it away!" he stammered, then stepped back, shocked by his own boldness. He'd always followed a simple policy regarding the city's homeless population: for him they would not exist. He wouldn't talk to them; he wouldn't even see them.

The beggar's grin cast a yellow glow over the lower part of her face. She couldn't have looked more frightening if she'd transformed into some sort of animal. And the stench, like half a dozen things dying in her mouth. "A simple coin, sir? It's all I ask. Little trouble for you, yet such great benefits will it bring to me."

For pity's sake. He almost laughed at the ridiculousness of her statement: what good would a quarter or a dime do her? She couldn't even buy a candy bar for that.

But still he found himself reaching into his pocket, pulling out what jingled there: a quarter, two quarters, a dime and a few pennies. He shoved them into her outstretched palm and turned to escape. But she grabbed his wrist, her hand a claw-like thing malformed by layers of callous and stain, and to his amazement pulled him to her, and pulled him into the alley behind, where in the darkness she surrounded him with her rank lips and sour laughter and reeking thighs, and took him out of his own head for an unknown period of time.

And when he struggled his way back, she lay dead at his feet, rags torn away and bits of cloth scattered like flesh after a predator's feast, and he saw how lovely she had been under her rags, and wondered how she could have influenced him to do such a terrible thing.

He could not think of such things for long; there was too much to do. He picked up her body—acutely aware that her smell had subsided, that in death she smelled rather pleasantly—and struggled with it into the darkest recess of the alley, where torn boxes and cloth all the colors of mud and a range of garbage resided, where some awful creature might have made its nest, and laid her there, and covered her with what was available, even though it repulsed him to have his hands in such filth.

He made his way out of there as quickly as he could and did not look back.

The smell of fingers was the absolute worst, because they were what touched the world most often and delved into the quiet, hidden places of your body. Sometimes he saw people sniffing their fingers upon exiting public restrooms. Some of them actually appeared to take satisfaction in what they were smelling.

He supposed feet were second, encased in their cloth tubing all day, falling asleep and dreaming of better places to go.

• • •

For the next few days, Riley treated his memory of the incident with the same distance and detachment he applied to all things of these odiferous streets. In a place the size of this city, events were occurring at all times, stories were being made, individual dramas were playing and replaying at a bewildering rate. Life in the city was like television: you turned it on and left it on for hours at a time, while you ate, while you talked on the phone, while you made love. You paid no more attention to one program than any other. It was all background noise.

Once, while waiting for a bus near the spot of the incident with the beggar, he had a stray thought that at least with her gone there might be one less foul smell to contend with. Testing his theory, he sniffed. In fact the city appeared to smell worse than ever.

Living in the city, Riley had found it necessary to shower two and three times daily simply to wash away the grime before it interacted with everyday bodily secretions to create a smell. He tried out various kinds of body scrapers, every variety of loofa. Sometimes his skin bled. It was amazing how deep the filth could go. Even after hours of scraping, he could rub his thumb across the back of his heel and a little pellet of skin and dirt and smell would appear like some sort of spontaneous egg. An egg of smell, smell made solid.

Sometimes he was so aware of the smells that he forgot to speak, and people thought him rude. But when the smells were at their strongest there was no need for words.

Riley traveled from restaurant to restaurant for his meals, tried not to repeat himself. He distrusted them all but figured he was less likely to receive a fatal dose of food poisoning if he avoided repeat dining. He liked to travel by alley, which he supposed was actually the dirtiest route a person could take, but gave him a chance to check out the dumpster of the restaurant he intended to eat in before entering the door. That way if he found some insurmountable violation of cleanliness—say the carcass of a cancerous cow—he could simply avoid that particular restaurant.

He met her that way on his way to lunch. He had been peering inside the dumpster just as she was climbing out: wrapped in rags so greasy they stuck to her body like diseased patches of skin. She was a young thing, not much out of her teens. He could see as much from her eyes and mouth: they took him all in hungrily, quickly.

Do me for a dime? She said it so softly she must have been in his head, sneaky about it so that he didn't notice her climb in.

It was a miserable hot day. They were tarring the roof next door and the workers had left their tar machine, their kettle of tar or whatever it was called, cooking in the alley a few dozen feet from the back entrance of the restaurant and this dumpster she'd peeled out of like a nymph from a bloom. She'd pulled him to a wall halfway between, like halfway between the moon and the sun, and she'd leaned against the bricks and opened herself up from the middle and pushed him inside. And he had to admit it was cool there and surprisingly soft but then the stench of her rolled itself out and climbed onto his face and would not let go. He'd cried and then he'd slapped and then folded her as if he could seal her in an envelope and mail her away. By the time he was done with her all he could really do was slip her into that vat of tar.

She had that unmistakable aroma of fried food. Fried food was the worst for you, he supposed, the worst smell because it was that burning animal fat smell. And he thought about fast food chicken and the awful smell of it and recognized this for the proof of what a foul group we are, just rancid animal fat and not really much more than that.

• • •

In some ways the smell of hair was the strangest, so dependent on the particular hair care products the person used. He imagined sometimes that this was the smell of raw thought, bits of it trapped in the hair fibers as the rest made its way up toward heaven.

The back of the neck was another foul-smelling region, the place where the collar rubs, a drainage basin for the hair hanging above. You could scrub there all you wanted and it would never be clean.

You rub and rub all day at your skin to remove the soiled skin and the sour-smelling sweat. You mine the stench. You can't help yourself.

One day the rain came and it was glorious in its unexpectedness. For a time at least the stench got washed out of the air. Riley could not quite describe what was left behind, what that quality was, but it was an absence of human animal scent, a kind of vague metallic scent, and for him it was glorious. Even his own poor skin smelled like the rain.

Such a reprieve cannot last forever, of course, and soon enough returned the smells of the machinery human beings shared the city with: the aromas and diesel, poorly processed exhausts and spontaneous mechanical belchings.

Then the people: their badly washed bodies and foods only partially digested. Their cigarette smoke and the sour taste of their breath wrapped around a pattern of daily insults.

Then another sudden downpour, and everything seemed blessedly right again.

But eventually the good effects of that rain passed as well, and a foul smell began to issue from the narrow strips of land between the tall buildings: the city mud.

• • •

She had come to him out of another downpour, pushing a grocery cart overloaded with plastic garbage bags and paper sacks. Pushing it for all she was worth so that she barely avoided running him down as she turned into the empty lot. At first Riley couldn't imagine what shelter could be found there, the lot was empty as far as he could see. Then he detected a bulge in a layer of trash near the center of the lot, a rise like a pitcher's mound. He watched her from behind some bushes as she unloaded the cart and stowed it in a shadowed corner of the lot. With her new things—indistinguishable, he thought, from the trash littering the ground—she approached the small mound.

With her rotting tennis shoes she scraped at the trash until a square of board appeared. She set down her new things and lifted the square from one edge as if it were a basement hatch.

Then, to his amazement, she walked down into the ground, pulling the board and trash back above her to hide the entrance.

Riley watched the bag lady for several days. He always kept his distance, not just to prevent exposure but because her stench was worse each day. Even though it continued to rain so hard and long the streets were flooding, the rain did not lessen her smell. Finally, when he thought she could be no riper, he watched her descend into her underground lair once again, then went over to her board and lifted it. There was no chamber here, just a shallow trench filled with trash. The bag lady lay on her back at its center, as if sleeping in her own future grave.

It's about time, I have been waiting so long. The words bubbled off her filthy lips, each one an exhalation of foulness.

Without thinking, he lay upon her, and after a time could not distinguish the stink of her body from the stink of her clothes or from the garbage she had made her bed with. As he wept his hands caressed and squeezed.

Over the next few months, Riley returned to the lot, lifted up the board, and checked on the progress of the body's decomposition. The weather continued uncharacteristically wet. Her clothes and eccentric bedding became exotic vegetables in a rancid soup that filled the trench. The stench became unbearable at times, and yet no neighbors complained, the police were not called, the body remained where he had left it.

City dwellers were used to bad smells; this was nothing unusual for them.

Riley could not say when he stopped bathing, but if you'd asked him why he might have told you it was so that he could better fit in.

After a time, he might say, you cannot tell if the stench is yours or if it comes from everyone else.

When they finally arrested Riley it was not for murder, or for any of a number of other violent acts he had committed over the last several years. They arrested Riley for an egregious number of sanitation violations, for a mound of rotting legal orders he had ignored, then dragged into his apartment to add to the malodorous nest that had become his home.

The police were alarmed when copious amounts of blood were found streaked through this nest, but later it was discovered that the blood was Riley's own. His arms, legs, and torso were seriously scarred with many poorly-healed wounds. "Fresh blood has this clean, coppery smell," he would later tell a doctor at the hospital. "You know, when it first hits the air. You can't smell anything else, at least for a few seconds."

"And what is it you're afraid of smelling, Mr. Riley?" the clever young doctor inquired.

"Why, it's the cooking, the cleaning, the smell of fear. The freshly-shampooed baby's head, the honey in the lover's kiss, the aroma, the perfume, the reek. It is the sour bouquet of the body as the organs begin to fail. It is the sadness of when we know what is to come, what is waiting for us when our last foul breath has spread through the room.

"Can't you smell it, doctor? It is the stench."

THE CRUSHER

He'd never had any luck with soft things. Even when he was a kid, his hands had been so big they'd just mashed things up, no matter how hard he tried to hold them steady, no matter how hard he tried to hold them in the same gentle way he loved them. The harder he tried the worse it was. The harder he tried the more things he broke.

Even words. He tried to hold them gently in his mouth but they always spilled out broken.

"Damn damn damn..." That was the way he'd told Alice how much he loved her. "Damn damn damn," with tears in his eyes. Alice just looked at him as if he were somebody who was always going around breaking things. And, of course, that was true. That was what he was.

But that wasn't everything he was.

He got into the business because of his arm wrestling. At every bar in the northwest that had such a contest, he'd show up to arm wrestle. That was his specialty, his only talent. He had a grip that made flesh shrink and bones fold, and nobody wanted to hold hands with him.

He'd never held Alice's hand. He'd been too afraid. She'd had a hand like a little bird and he'd broken more than a few birds when he was a kid. And hamsters. And kittens. And he'd loved them all. So he wasn't about to hold Alice's hand, whom he loved most of all.

Of course, he won every arm wrestling competition he entered. That was how he first came to the attention of the promoter. He'd broken some fellow's arm up above Portland, and it made the local papers. The fellow hadn't pressed charges or anything like that—in fact he'd told the reporters how much he admired the strength, the skill it took.

But he knew there wasn't any skill involved. Mashing things. Crushing things. He would have stopped it if he could. But he just didn't have the control.

"James," she whispered. "James don't go." It was Alice's voice, all right, and Alice was the only one called him James. To everybody else he was Jim, or Big Jim, when they used his name at all. To most people, he guessed, he didn't even have a name.

Except she'd never told him not to go. Nothing like that. That was just something his heart told him. What she'd really said, he'd crushed out of his mind forever.

"A guy like you, you can make some money." That was all that wrestling promoter said, really, pretty much said the same thing over and over. Just used different words for it. The promoter kept trying to build up his ego, not knowing that that didn't matter much to him. But he needed to make a living, so he signed, and that made the promoter very happy.

They billed him as "The Crusher," a name he didn't care for, but he also didn't care enough to get the promoter to change it. Before every match he'd crush something for the audience: a few oil cans, a steel trashcan, sometimes cantaloupes or melons that made a satisfying mess. He hated to admit to feeling the satisfaction, but it was there.

And now entering the ring, The Crusher! A thunder of boos, with scattered cheers, the cheers increasing with each bout. That's what he liked best about professional wrestling: the frame of cheers and boos, the dancing around that went in between. If only those cheers and boos would follow him out of the ring, rise up like music at important points in the rest of his life, he'd feel a lot more comfortable about moving around with other people. Not happy exactly—happy was a word they used in bad movies and stupid TV shows. He'd figured that much out at least. But comfortable, the way most people are comfortable walking around being the way people are supposed to be. He'd never had that, but he'd like to.

And now entering the ring... He pushed down on the bottom rope and stepped through. Then he walked around the ring a couple of times, reaching out his hands to slap his opponent's hands, pulling back quickly as if he was touching fire. Pretty much every match started that way because that was the way the promoter wanted it. Slap and dance, circle and tease, then the first hard embrace: his opponent pressing his body full into him, and the Crusher thinking it was like some play, or some movie, and that gave him the butterflies so bad he could hardly breathe.

Then his opponent would get away, or, rather, The Crusher would release him, and there would be more dancing, and making faces, and doing these things with the eyes, kind of like two little boys in a playground, which is what the crowd really wanted to see, two little boys in a playground, even though they might not know it. The crowds didn't want to see somebody really get hurt, even though that was the way it might look sometimes. But Jim could see right through that, and it kind of made him feel good about people. Although that never lasted too long.

So he tried to give the crowd what they really wanted. The dance and the tease, the tickle, and several hard embraces with dances in between. Then finally The Crusher, both his name and what he did at the same time. "Crush-er! Crush-er!" the crowd would shout, and they were calling out his name, but they were also telling him what to do, telling him how to end it. And he always obliged. He wrapped his arms around his partner and crushed, but he always held himself back a little. These were big guys up against him, but he still had to hold himself back. Lots of times they would pass out, and he'd step back a little, holding on to them with one hand so they wouldn't hit the canvas too hard.

Sometimes a rib would end up getting cracked, and that always made him feel really bad. Then the next time in the ring he'd be too easy, and it wouldn't be convincing, and the promoter would get mad, and then the time after that he'd squeeze harder, and it would be too hard and the guy would get hurt, and then Jim, aka The Crusher, would be miserable again.

He first started seeing the girl in the crowd up in Washington State. She was thin and pale, with hair so blonde it looked white under the lights. She was there at every match, and once he almost killed a fellow because he caught on to how intensely she was staring at him, and he found himself staring back, rock still with his arms around this guy, and before he knew it a couple of his wrestling buddies were there in the ring with him, trying to pry his arms from around the man's gut.

He didn't wrestle for awhile after that, didn't even show up to watch. He'd take these long walks in the woods and he'd be so full of aches he'd think he'd pulled every muscle in his body. But he hadn't pulled a thing, and no amount of heat or ointment was going to fix him. Sometimes he'd find a good-sized tree and wrap his arms around that, squeeze and crush and pretend he was pulling the thing out of the ground roots and all, and then sometimes the aching would go away.

The girl showed up again at a match in northern California. She looked the same but more so, her eyes noticeably red even from the ring, as if she'd been doing nothing but crying since the last time he saw her. That wasn't likely, he thought, but the fantasy made him smile a little. He never thought of himself as having fans.

She was at every match in San Francisco, and he saw her at all the cities and towns all the way down the coast. That first night in San Diego she was waiting for him outside when he left the dressing room.

"Mr. Crusher," she said, shyly, like a schoolgirl. It made

him laugh, and then he saw this uncertain look cross her face and he felt bad.

"Jim. It's my real name."

"Sure." She had inched closer, but he edged away. For some reason he was scared of this small and lovely person.

"I saw you wrestle tonight," she said.

And dozens of times before, he thought, but said nothing.

"You're very... strong," she said. "It's like you could break anything... that bothered you."

"Some things you can't break."

"It's like you could just crush it out of existence," she said, as if she hadn't heard him, and looking into her eyes he could tell she hadn't. "You're strong enough... you could just make it not be."

He was embarrassed now. And he wanted her to stop saying what she was saying. "Do you want me to sign a picture or something?" he asked and immediately felt himself redden. Now she would think he was some sort of arrogant would-be celebrity. Some of the guys did think of themselves as celebrities, but Jim didn't.

"If you want. But I would really like to take you out to dinner, if that's okay with you."

"I..." Jim couldn't figure out what to do with his hands. Finally he let them grip and wrestle each other. "I usually . . ."

"I don't know anyone here," she said. "And I really find it depressing to eat by myself."

Jim surprised himself by agreeing, even though the very idea terrified him. But telling this woman no, after the things she had just said to him, would have mortified him even more.

They took her car. Jim didn't drive—steering wheels had never felt right in his hands.

It wasn't until they got to the restaurant that Jim wondered how he was going to eat in front of this sweet young thing. He always ate alone, and almost never in restaurants. Sometimes when the bus stopped and the other wrestlers all went in to eat, together around some long table, Jim would order something to go, then eat it on the bus. Sometimes he would stare out the bus window, and into the restaurant where the others were, and pretend he was eating with them.

It was his hands, of course, that made him unsuitable for public dining. There was no way those massive hands and forearms could hold a fork delicately, or use a knife without bumping into the person next to him or sending his own food flying across the table. And those thick, long fingers of his were always getting in the way. They were like wandering roots, and he had no control over them. Sometimes he wouldn't watch them for awhile, then glance down and they'd be wriggling in secret, anxious to touch and break something.

So he struggled through the meal and actually ate very little, dropping some of it on the floor, some into his lap. Finally so hungry he could have cried, he picked up a pork chop and stuffed the meaty side into his mouth, using the bone as a handle. He closed his eyes while he did this, not wanting to see her look at him. But she never said anything about it, or seemed to notice. Mostly, she talked about herself.

"My dad has this junk car lot outside Eugene," she went on. "Andy's, but that's not his name. I don't know who Andy is, or even if there ever was one. The place is full of rusted hulks, mostly, but he refuses to clean up the place or haul anything out of there. He always says he's going to fix them up, even the ones so rusted through they don't have floors anymore, and the seats are full of wild flowers. He lives there full-time in this shack. We moved out there when I was twelve, after my mom died."

Jim put the piece of pork chop down, edged the plate away as if he could pretend he'd never seen it before. "I'm . . . sorry," he said, and immediately felt stupid, clumsy. She'd been twelve. It was a long time ago. It was probably dumb for him to say "sorry" now.

But she didn't seem to have heard him. "I used to watch him move pieces of cars and trucks around. He was big, like you. And he didn't say much, like you. Like most of the wrestlers

I've met, I guess." He looked at her then, and when she saw that she acted suddenly nervous. "Well, I know you've seen me around the circuit. I go to lots of matches, especially when I see certain wrestlers and what they can do, well, I guess I follow them around to see what more they can do."

Jim had no idea what she was talking about. He really wished he could eat some more, just to have something to do with his mouth and hands. He tried folding his hands together on the table, but didn't know quite what to do with his overstuffed fingers. "Some of the wrestlers... they have lots of fans," he said awkwardly.

"Oh... oh, I'm sure they do," she said with a little wink that made Jim have to look away. "I know you have your fans, too. I've seen how the people look at you, especially the women."

Jim felt his face fill with blood. He was suddenly dizzy, and squeezed the edge of the table until he heard a cracking noise. Then he jerked his hand away, trying to focus on the fact that he was in a restaurant, where ordinary, real-life people spent their time. He tried to look at her and smile, let her know that everything was okay and that he could be perfectly normal. But he couldn't get his eyes up. He found himself staring at her plate, her hands and arms. And then he saw where her sleeve had ridden up, and all the scars it had been hiding.

"I was going to tell you about those," she said softly. He was a little alarmed that she could tell where he was looking. "I don't want to hide anything from you... Jim. I'd never want to keep secrets from you."

Jim still didn't look into her eyes. What was she talking about? He felt like some fellow in a movie—women just didn't talk to him this way. "It's okay..." he mumbled, not understanding, and not knowing what else to say.

"My dad was a very lonely man after my mother died. He wasn't good with other people, never had been." Just like me, Jim thought. The idea made him nervous. "I was pretty lonely, too, living out there with him. We didn't have a TV, and I never understood much about things, never had friends to compare the things that were happening to me. But for all I didn't understand, I was growing up pretty fast. Do you understand what I'm telling you, Jim?"

"No..." he said with a shock, as if the very idea of his understanding was impossible to imagine.

She leaned closer. "It was like I was his wife, Jim. We had sex." She had no expression on her face. He couldn't understand that. Why was she telling him things he couldn't possibly understand? "I thought giving to him was what I was supposed to do. I just wanted to make him be okay. But he took everything." She grabbed his wandering fingers and squeezed them together in her hand. He was surprised by how much it hurt. "Everything..."

"I...I wish that hadn't happened. I wish I..."

"You can help me, Jim. I knew from the first time I saw you in the ring that you could help me."

He thought she was going to drive him back to the motel where the promoter and the rest of the wrestlers were staying. She'd asked him where he was staying, and he told her, but she didn't drive him anywhere near there. She drove him to another motel, a smaller one further out. When she pulled up in front of a room and turned off the ignition, she said to him, "You're going to help me, Jim."

Jim knew it wasn't a question. And she had no right driving him out there and not telling him where they were going—he knew that much. But it didn't make him mad. He didn't think he could ever be mad at someone like her. Not just because he liked her. But because she scared him, too.

He followed her into the room, and when she told him to take off his clothes, he did. And when she told him to get into bed with her, he did. But when she told him to hold her, to make love to her, he hesitated.

"You told me you would help me," she said softly. He could barely see her face in the dark of the room, but he felt her all over his skin. "You promised, Jim."

His hands were trembling. He didn't know what to do with them. "I'm scared," he whispered.

"I know you are, sweetheart. But you're going to help me. Hold me, Jim. I can't do this unless you hold me. I've tried everything I can think of. I need this real bad."

So he slipped his arms carefully around her, trembling as he touched the soft smallness of her, afraid of his own clumsy fingers, afraid of his huge hands. She was a glass doll he had to carry somewhere, and he was scared because she hadn't told him where yet. "Tell me," he said. "Please tell me."

"Hold me a little tighter, Jim. I can't feel you enough. Hold me." And when he still hesitated she started doing things with her hands, stroking his chest, wiggling down under him to rub his groin. She was suddenly everywhere, and he had to reach to catch her, to hold her. "Tighter, Jim . . . tighter . . ."

"I want to . . . I can't . . ."

". . . tighter . . . what I need . . ."

Then it was over. Maybe it had been over for minutes and he hadn't noticed. He couldn't be sure. What surprised him most was that he hadn't heard the bones breaking, or realized when she'd stopped telling him to hold her tighter. He cried for a long time, and then finally he was mad at her. Furious. She'd gotten exactly what she wanted, but did she ever think about what it would do to him?

It took a couple of weeks for him to get to her father's junk yard. He had to take the back roads, and he hitched a ride only when he thought it was pretty safe.

Of course her father was dead. At least five years, according to the man who had taken over the place. Jim wasn't surprised. "You sure are a big one," the man said, and Jim just nodded. "Need a job?" And of course Jim took it. Besides the other considerations, he had to eat.

He could wrestle a whole car by himself if he took his time. And ripping things out, breaking things, that was easy enough.

He liked the dance he did with a big piece of rusted steel up in his arms, raised toward the sky like a gift. The owner would laugh and shake his head and say he'd never seen anybody so strong. "You're a regular super duper hero," he said. "The Muscleman. The Bruiser."

But Jim knew he was The Crusher, and always would be. When the owner went home at night, Jim stayed behind in the little falling-down shack. Then in the middle of the night he would walk and pick up the sharpest pieces of ragged steel he could find, and hold them, embrace them, crush them into his chest where they made scars that tangled and grew into the most beautiful and complex design he had ever seen.

And she would watch, and tell him, tell him how strong he was.

LIVING ARRANGEMENT

Monte had never been a good father, in fact he had been pretty lousy by anyone's standards, but after he lost his job and became too ill to work and the arthritis made it so he could hardly move his legs, his daughter pretended otherwise and asked him to come live with her, her young son, and the current boyfriend. "You always took care of me," she said. "Let me do this for you."

That wasn't true, not by a long shot—he'd had shit to do with her upbringing. He'd left all that to her mother and he'd been gone half the time and the half the time he was there he'd made them all miserable including himself.

But he accepted her offer. What else was he supposed to do? He didn't know why she was lying to him, or if she was just lying to herself about him. Nor did he particularly care. He had to survive somehow. Or did he? That was one of those questions that got harder to answer every year.

His little corner of her house was a closet of a room at the back, just off the porch and the kitchen. In a fancier house it might have been called the mud room. A battery-powered radio. One box for his toiletries. One box for his miscellaneous. A mail slot of a window let some light in. It was a lot better than he deserved. He actually couldn't remember if he'd hit her when she was a kid, but he probably had. He didn't remember a lot from those days. She could have been a little yippy dog running around for all he could recall of her childhood.

He had a single bed, and she made him strip it and hand her the sheets for the wash. If it had been up to him he'd have let the sheets go yellow, then brown, then replace them. Monte discovered he liked the look, and the smell, of wet sheets flapping in the wind. Old age was full of surprises.

She didn't expect anything from him, or at least that's what she said. He got a small social security check every month which he just signed over to her, leaving it under the peanut butter jar in the pantry. They never talked about it, but those checks got cashed.

He had no use for spending money. He used to drink. About fifteen years ago he stopped, and he couldn't have told you why. One day he just woke up and decided he didn't care to anymore. It might not be permanent—he reserved the right to start up again at any time. Maybe if this living with family thing didn't work out. And he'd been a smoker until recently, quitting cold turkey when he moved in with her. He actually liked the discomfort the craving for it gave him. It kept him focused.

For entertainment he read old paperbacks people threw away; he didn't care which ones. He never turned on the TV. Almost everything on it seemed stupid to him, including the news. When the boy turned on the cartoons and Monte was in the living room, he either left the room or made himself fall asleep. Falling asleep was easy—it was the waking up that was hard.

His daughter had had a lot of boyfriends. He made himself not think about that too much. He was no one to judge, but she had a history of making bad choices. Maybe she learned that from him. It made life pretty hard sometimes. And possibly dangerous. None of his business, but she had a kid to think of.

Pete, the current boyfriend, wasn't there much, either working late, or out hitting the bars, doing the kind of things guys of that age and type usually do. Guys like Pete didn't have much going for them. Monte had been a guy like Pete, pretty much. Monte guessed if he were healthier, he'd still be a guy like Pete. Monte guessed it was a good thing Pete was gone so much. He also guessed Pete was cheating on her. Something about the way Pete was when he came in late, the way he kissed her. And the way Pete talked about how much he'd had to do that day—just a little too eager. Monte recognized that particular performance. Shit, he practically invented it. Most men were terrible liars, transparent as hell. The only way a woman could buy such crap was because she wanted to. He figured his daughter was just desperate for the company. If she truly believed Pete's garbage, well then, she was worse off than Monte thought.

Monte could also see that Pete had a dangerous side. He just didn't know how dangerous. He watched the two of them together, even when they probably thought he was sleeping. They had arguments, some of them bad. Hearing his daughter cursing and shouting at her man made Monte angry, but he wasn't sure why. It was none of his business. And Pete sure deserved it. But she was aggravating Pete. Things were okay for now—there was a balance going on, but that could end any time. Monte had seen some bad things. But maybe this would be okay.

If they got too loud, Monte would just turn up his radio. Everybody had a messy life. She didn't need Monte to defend her—she knew what she was getting into. He'd never met her boy's father, but he didn't need to. Monte reckoned he was the same kind of guy as Pete. One thing Monte knew about women—they stuck with what they knew.

The boy, his grandson, was a quiet boy, and a good boy. Seven years old. A great age, from the little Monte could remember. Monte had had a dog when he was about that age. Monte tried not to say too much to the boy because he was afraid he'd fuck him up. He didn't want to tell the boy it was all downhill from here—maybe it would turn out different for him. Monte didn't believe it would, but sometimes things surprised him.

"Take off those jeans and let me mend them," she said to the boy and the boy did as she asked without saying a word. The three of them were in the living room, Monte pretending to read the paper but he was actually more interested in his daughter's and the boy's conversation. The truth was there was never much interesting in the paper, just people behaving badly and he knew all he wanted to know about that.

The boy wore white Pooh underpants with red trim. His T-shirt had a picture of a honey pot on it. It looked kind of sissy but Monte didn't say anything.

His daughter sewed the tear in the left knee slowly and carefully using small stitches. Monte wondered if she'd learned that from her mother. "It's important that no matter how poor you are you don't go running around wearing torn clothes," his daughter told the boy. "Your grandpa taught me that. He wouldn't let his kids run around in torn clothes, no sir." She glanced at Monte then and he nodded at her. She'd made the whole thing up. Monte considered whether she could have learned that from her mother as well.

He thought about the boy—"his grandson" was the way somebody might say it. Somebody might ask him, "Is that your grandson?" and he'd have to say, "Yes." He couldn't say why exactly, but that was a pretty big deal. It surprised him that he could feel that way. But he couldn't stop thinking about the boy. He wondered if that meant he loved the boy. He didn't like thinking about that, it embarrassed him to think about that, but he couldn't help himself. It made him feel weak, but he'd been feeling weak for a very long time now, so maybe it didn't make any difference that he was weak. Weak was still better than dead, most of the time.

"Dad, why don't you tell Brian a goodnight story?"

"A goodnight story?"

"Brian, your grandpa is a great storyteller. When we were little he told us stories every night to help us go to sleep."

Why are you lying like this you stupid bitch? But Monte didn't say anything out loud. Brian walked slowly over to Monte's chair and sat down on the dark blue rug in front of him. The boy gazed up at him, waiting. Monte figured the boy must have heard lots of goodnight stories before and this was the way he'd been taught to listen to them.

Monte said to his daughter, "I don't know any stories."

"Sure you do, Dad. Everybody knows some stories."

The boy, his grandson, was still waiting. Monte frowned down at the boy, not knowing what to do. Monte started clearing his throat because something was there, something was in there bothering him.

Then he just began talking. "A long time back, when I was just a young man." He stopped and spoke to the boy. "I'm not going to say 'Once upon a time.' Is that okay by you?"

The boy said nothing and Monte took that for a yes. "I was older than you, Brian. But I didn't have a wife yet, or kids. I was a teenager, I guess." He glanced over at his daughter, who was watching him so seriously he felt embarrassed and angry, so he looked away. "I never thought I'd have kids. I never thought much of anything, past the particular day. I was never a planner." He stopped.

The boy appeared to be listening intently, but Monte knew he'd already screwed up. This was no way to tell a kid's story.

"But I had a serious problem. I guess you could say I had a giant problem." Monte felt himself dripping with sweat. But the kid seemed more interested. "There was a giant in my life, tall as a house, wide as a four lane highway. And that giant, he was always getting in my way, hassling me. He never had a good word to say about me, or anybody else. And if you objected to anything he said, you'd get the back of his hand, broad as an elephant's backside, right in your face. Some times he'd hit you so hard you'd be flying right into—"

He paused, glanced at his daughter, who was staring at him. He couldn't tell if she approved or disapproved of his story—most likely she didn't much care for it. But she'd asked for it, hadn't she?

"You'd be flying right into Never-Never land. Leastways, I think that's what they called it. Anyway, this went on for some years. Some days the giant would be nice as pie. Apple Pie, I reckon, since that was always my favorite. But most days he was just this big monster of a thing you'd best stay away from. And on the worst days he would chase me around the house and when I got mad about that he'd say I was really in for it. He'd say he had special plans for me that I wasn't going to like at all. Well, I had seen some examples of his special plans, and no sir, they weren't nice things for anybody to have to go through."

Monte looked at his daughter again, thinking Okay, you wanted me to do this. See what happened? But he couldn't tell at all what she was thinking, which was really no surprise. He wondered if he'd gone too far, but the boy didn't look scared. The boy seemed very interested.

"That was when I knew I had to do something. I had to do something to protect myself. Of course, killing is a bad thing, an evil thing. It's something a person should only do when they have to, to protect themselves or the ones they…they love."

Monte stopped, trying to think out the rest of the story. He knew his daughter was watching him closely, but he avoided eye contact.

"But it's okay to kill an evil giant, isn't it? If I remember right, that's what Jack did in his story. Well, in my story I knew I had to do pretty much the same thing. I was small for my age. A lot like you, Brian. I was a tough little beggar, but I wouldn't say I was strong. There's a difference. No, I wasn't what you would call strong.

"But you don't have to be strong to kill a giant, Brian. You don't even have to be big. You just have to be. Persistent, that's the word for what you have to be. That means you have to keep trying. You keep at it and you keep at it until finally that job is done.

"So I was persistent, Brian. That giant drank a lot. I think a lot of giants drink a lot. Giants just have giant appetites, I guess. And one night that giant drank so much he fell fast asleep. And then I saw my chance. I went into the kitchen. I was still in my pajamas. I went into the kitchen and I opened the drawer and I found a giant knife. A giant knife for a giant." Monte tried to laugh but it sounded fake. It sounded high and strangled and not like his regular laugh at all. "And I took that giant knife and I carried it into the giant's bedroom. The giant snored like most giants, so loud it made the walls and floors and my own chest shake. It even made my hands shake.

"Then I climbed up on the giant's bed with the knife and I just kept at it. I kept at it and I kept at it until that giant was dead. End of story."

Monte glanced down at the boy and saw that he was asleep on the floor. And he didn't look worried. If anything it appeared he had a little smile on his face. Monte's daughter went over and picked up the boy and carried him into his bedroom.

When his daughter got back she said, "That was quite a story, Dad."

"I think you must have heard some of that story before. Maybe from your mother."

"Maybe," she replied. "Why did you tell him that story, anyway?" She averted her gaze.

Can't look me in the eye, Monte thought. "Don't do that, honey," he said.

She appeared surprised. Monte tried to remember if he'd ever called her "honey" before. He didn't think so. He figured that's what surprised her.

"What are you talking about?"

"I think you know that's my only story, the only one I have to tell. I think you knew it was my only story when you asked me to tell him one. I think the question should be why you wanted me to tell him that story."

Pete got home during the middle of the night. Monte didn't

know what time—he had no watch or clock of any kind. He just woke up to a bunch of stomping, and cursing, and things getting knocked around, breaking.

He had to use the bathroom badly, but he didn't want to walk out there in the middle of all that. It wasn't like he could do it quickly and sneak back into bed. Everything took him a long time to do. He just hoped he wouldn't pee the bed again, or soak these old man pajamas that did a pretty good job of keeping him warm. The last time his daughter didn't say a word—just took the wet sheets out of his hands and went to wash them. It shamed him something terrible, but she could have made it worse and didn't.

But the yelling and the throwing went on another half-hour or more, and Monte was fit to burst. His daughter was crying and he could ignore that, or almost, but he couldn't ignore his bladder. He crawled out of bed as quick as he could, but already he could feel himself leaking a little. So he redoubled his efforts to hold it in, shuffling down the hall toward the bathroom all bent over like he was a hundred years old.

Monte didn't intend to look at anything, just make a bee-line for that bathroom, that is, if the bee was old and arthritic and the slowest bee that still lived. But he was a little confused by the hall, and the shadows, and all the noise. So he found himself peeking into doorways as he passed, trying to remember where the bathroom was, and that's when he saw Pete standing in the living room, his daughter lying on the floor with her mouth bleeding, and little Brian standing on the other side of the room, wedged into the corner, crying, a big red mark tearing down one side of his face.

"Well, if it ain't the man of leisure!" Pete called drunkenly. "You best get on with what you were doing, old man!"

Monte's groin buzzed with the pain. But he stopped, thinking about it. Was he just going to go on down to the bathroom and pee? And then what? What could he say when he got back? Or would he just hide out in the bathroom until it was all over? Hell of a thing. He gazed at Brian, who had his hands up over his face now, but still watching with one shocked white eye. Right then the only sound in the room was his daughter's torn breathing.

Monte shuffled a couple of feet into the room, still bent over. To his alarm, he began to cry from the pain.

"Hey, old man, what did I tell you? I pay for the roof over your head—you realize that, don't you? I pay for both of them, too. Why do you think she's here? Because I pay! She's a whore and he's just a bastard!"

Monte, still bent over, spit on the floor. "You're not even worth their shit," he said.

Monte didn't see it coming, but he felt the thunder of it. Suddenly he was on the floor, his side and his back on fire from a series of Pete's clumsy but enraged blows. He thought he could feel the blood pooling out under him, then realized he'd pissed himself. He turned his head to the side to avoid the spreading wet stink, which allowed him to watch Pete take a swift kick into his daughter's side as he passed her, on his way to grabbing Brian—hysterical now—by the arm and jerking him into the bedroom. Monte lay perfectly still as the piss spread to his cheek, watching through the open bedroom door as Pete stripped the boy naked and beat on him with a belt. There might have been worse, but he couldn't see it all, so he tried not to think that far. He closed his eyes.

The odd thing was, in the past Monte might have fantasized what he was going to do to Pete later, if he could have. At least he would be figuring out who he could call, who might do the job for next to no money. Monte didn't know men like that anymore, but he knew there were always men like that.

But those fantasies were bullshit. He'd never find anybody. Nobody was going to do anything like that for him anymore. Nobody was taking him seriously about a damn thing.

So he thought about things he could do. And Monte thought maybe he could kill the boy. Monte was old and weak but he could still probably kill a seven year old boy. If he was determined enough. If it would save that boy some of the pains seven-year-olds had no business to know but that Monte knew all about.

Monte woke up the next morning in his bed, naked, feeling like he'd fallen down a rocky mountainside. When he moved he felt a sharp pain near his left shoulder blade, but he discovered that if he held his body a certain way, keeping that shoulder slightly back behind the rest of him, he could sit up and swing his legs around without too much pain. He had a vague memory of picking himself up, like picking up an armful of broken branches, and wandering down the hall, finding his room, fumbling with the light switch, stripping out of his stinking pajamas and boxers, leaving them on the floor just inside the door, as far away from the bed as he could think of. Crawling under the blankets so carefully, thinking that something was going to tear open if he wasn't as careful as he could possibly be.

He didn't think he had turned off his bedroom light. But it was off now, and what appeared to be his cleaned pajamas and boxers lay neatly folded on top of the dresser, along with some towels, a basin of water, wash cloths, giant bar of soap, a big bottle of peroxide.

It took awhile to clean himself up, and he didn't have a mirror, but he wasn't entering any pageants this year, so that would have to do. It took him even longer to get himself dressed, and he wasn't able to struggle into his shirt without some hellacious pain. But he managed. His daughter's message was pretty clear—in this house you took care of your damage before you left your bedroom. Then you put a smile on your face and you walked out the door.Which he did, more or less. What he wore on his face wasn't exactly a smile, but it would have to do.

His daughter was in the kitchen, bent over the sink, palms flat on the counter to either side. "You okay?" he asked.

"Sure." She spoke without turning. "Got to sleep a little late. We all did. Brian's still in bed."

His eyes found the wall clock. It was a Mexican-looking thing: brightly-painted clay rooster with a clock face in the center. It was after ten. "Brian's not going to school? And you're not going in to the restaurant?"

"Brian's feeling a little under the weather. I think we all could use a day off, don't you?"

Monte took it wrong at first. Man of leisure. Then he realized that wasn't the way she meant it. "Brian okay?"

"Sure. Brian'll be fine. Sit down, Dad. Let me make you some breakfast."

She jammed two pieces of bread into the toaster, broke two eggs on the edge of the skillet and got it sizzling, went searching through the fridge. "No fresh-squeezed OJ, Dad. An orange okay?" Her voice muffled, throaty.

"Sure. It's all great. Should I go say hello to Brian?"

"No, Dad. Just stay here and eat your breakfast."

She had mastered her mother's tone. She hadn't meant it as a suggestion. Monte sat with his elbows on the table, then moved them and folded his hands into his lap, while she dropped the eggs and toast onto a plate, filled a glass full of water, carried it all to the table, the orange balanced in the crook of her elbow.

He watched her as she placed everything on the placemat in front of him. The silverware had already been laid out on a perfectly folded napkin. Her neck had dark purple and green bruises on both sides, strangulation marks, a crust of blood just inside her right nostril.

"That looks bad," he said. "Where is he now?"

"Let's don't talk about it. He's still sleeping it off." She locked eyes with him. She had the look of a stern child, one too old for her years. She sat down across the table from him.

"I'll need a knife for the orange," he said.

"Oh. Sorry." She started to open a kitchen drawer, stopped. She left the kitchen, coming back minutes later with something wrapped in newspaper. She put it down beside his plate. "Happy birthday," she said.

He looked at the package, reluctant to touch it. "What makes you think it's my birthday?" he asked.

"Isn't it?" She seemed suddenly bored, or depressed.

"No. Not unless I forgot."

"It doesn't make any difference, Dad. Do you remember my birthday?"

He thought a few seconds, even though he knew what he was going to have to say. "No. But I remember the day you were born."

"Oh?" Still bored. "What was that like?"

"Scary. I'd never been that close to a baby. Didn't want to pick you up because I was afraid your arms might break off."

"That's stupid, Dad."

Maybe he should have taken offense at this, but he didn't. "Yeah. I was stupid. I just couldn't see the human being in you. If you were talking, maybe, but with you just making those baby sounds, and crying all the time, and needing God-knows-what to keep you alive, I just didn't know what to do with you."

"So you left."

"So I left." He stared at his food. "Sorry."

"Don't say you're sorry, Dad. Just unwrap your package so you can eat your orange."

He examined the newspaper, then tore it away. Inside was a wicked looking thing. "A hunting knife?" It wasn't really a question.

"Now you can cut your orange."

Monte kept thinking that wasn't the right way to use a good hunting knife, and this was a good one, he could tell. It had a polished bone handle, the blade shiny as a new car.

"Something wrong?"

"No, no it's great." He put the orange on the plate. The knife went through it like it wasn't there. Monte felt himself grin involuntarily, then stopped it. What was wrong with him? It was a silly present, he obviously had no use for it, but it excited him just the same.

"Good. Maybe you'll get some use out of it," she said, and

got up, grabbed the skillet and a scouring pad, started cleaning up.

Like he'd ever go hunting again, or fishing for that matter. She was a stupid girl. He didn't understand how that could be. His wife had been a smart woman. Maybe she got the stupid from him.

He thought about his daughter's present while he finished his breakfast, and he sat there for a while afterwards thinking about it while she continued to clean the kitchen. He didn't even know what she was cleaning anymore. It all appeared spotless to him. He thought about the boyfriend sleeping in the other room and he thought about his grandson and what he had considered doing to the boy. And he thought about his daughter bringing him here to live with her, saying how he had always taken care of her, when she knew full well he hadn't taken care of her at all. He thought about why in the world she'd want a man like him around when she already had a man too much like him in the other room sleeping it off. He thought about all of these things until he couldn't think anymore.

"Lacey," he said. She turned around, surprised. He knew she was surprised because he'd used her name, and he didn't do that often. "Lacey, I want you to wrap a scarf around your neck and take your son out for some ice cream. He'll feel better once he gets some ice cream in him."

His daughter watched him a few seconds, then she said, "Okay, Dad."

The boy was groggy and red-faced but wasn't unwilling to go. His jacket was too big for him and Monte thought his daughter really ought to do something about some better fitting clothes. Before they left, his grandson turned to him and waved. "Bye, Grandpa," he said. Monte raised his hand a bit. His daughter rushed the boy out without a backward glance.

Monte didn't know what was going to happen. You get past a certain age and it seems like you never know what's going to happen. He was old, and he was weak, but he could still lie down on top of somebody with a knife in his hand. He slowly made his way down the hall. He might be old but he was a tough old beggar. He was persistent. He'd stay at it and stay at it until the job got done.

JESSE

Jesse says he figures it's about time we did another one.

He uses "we" like we're Siamese twins or something, like we both decide what's going to happen and then it happens. Like we just do it, two bodies with one mind like in some weird movie. But it's Jesse that does it, all of it, each and every time. I'm just along for the ride. It's not my fault what Jesse does. I can't stop him—nobody could.

"Why?" I ask, and I feel bad that my voice has to shake, but I can't help it. "Why is it time, Jesse?"

"'Cause I'm afraid you're forgetting too many things, John. You're forgetting how we do it, and how they look."

We again. Like Jesse doesn't do a thing by himself. But Jesse does everything by himself. "I don't forget," I say.

"Oh, but I think you do. I know you do. It's time all right." Then he gets up from his nest in the sour straw and starts toward the barn door. And even though I haven't forgotten how they look, and how we do it, how he does it—how could anybody forget something like that?—I get up out of the straw and follow.

When Jesse called me up that day I didn't take him all that

seriously. Jesse was always calling me up and saying crazy things.

"Come on over," he said. "I gotta show you something."

I laughed at him. "You're in enough trouble," I said. "Your parents grounded you, remember? Two weeks at least, you told me."

"My parents are dead," he said, in his serious voice. But I had heard his serious voice a thousand times, and I knew what it meant.

I laughed. "Sure, Jesse. Deader than a flat frog on the highway, right?"

"No, deader than your dick, dickhead." He was always saying that. I laughed again. "Come on over. I swear it'll be okay."

"Okay. My mom has to go to the store. She can drop me off and pick me up later."

"No. Don't come with your mom. Take your bike."

"Christ, Jesse. It's five miles!"

"You've done it before. Take your bike or don't come at all."

"Okay. Be there when I get there." He made me mad all the time. All he had to do was tell me to do something and I'd do it. When I first knew him I did things he said because I felt sorry for him. His big brother had died when a tractor rolled over on him. I wasn't there but people said it was pretty awful. I heard my dad tell my mom that there must have been a dozen men around but none of them could do a thing. Jesse's brother had been awake the whole time, begging them to get the tractor off, that he could feel his heart getting ready to stop, that he knew it was going to stop any second. Dad said the blood was seeping out from under the tractor, all around his body, and Jesse's brother was looking at it like he just couldn't believe it. And Jesse was there watching the whole thing, Dad said. They couldn't get him to go away.

It gave me the creeps, what Jesse's brother had said. 'Cause I've always been afraid my heart was just going to stop some day, for no good reason. And to feel your heart getting ready to stop, that would be horrible.

Because of all that I felt real bad for Jesse, so for awhile there he would ask me to do something, anything, and I'd do it for him. I'd steal somebody's lunch or pull down a little kid's pants or walk across the creek on a little skinny board, all kinds of stupid crap. But after awhile I just did it because he said. He didn't make you want to feel bad for him. I wasn't even sure that he cared that his brother was dead. Once I asked him if he still felt bad about it and he just said that his brother picked on him all the time. That's all he would say about it. Jesse was always weird like that.

I hadn't ridden my bike in over a year—I wasn't sure I still could. I thought sixteen-year-olds were too old to ride bikes—guys were getting their licenses and were willing to walk or get rides with older friends until that day happened. And I was big for my age, a lot bigger than Jesse. I felt stupid. But I rode my bike the five miles anyway, just because Jesse told me to.

By the time I got to his farm I was so tired and mad I just threw the bike down in the gravel driveway. I didn't care if I broke it—I wasn't going to ride it home no matter what. Jesse came to the screen door with a smirk on his face. "Took you long enough," he said. "I didn't think you were coming."

"I'm here, all right? What'd you want to show me that was so damn important?"

He pulled me down the hall. He was so excited and it was happening so fast I was having a real bad feeling even before I saw them. He stopped in front of the door to his parents' bedroom and knocked it open with his fist. The sound made me jump. Then when I looked inside there were his parents on the floor, sleeping.

A short laugh came out of me like a bark. They looked silly: his mom's dress pulled up above her knees and his dad's mouth hanging open like he was drunk. They had their arms folded over their bellies. I never saw people sleeping that way before. The sheets and blankets and pillows had been pulled off the bed and were arranged around them and underneath them like a nest. His mom had never been a good housekeeper—

Jesse told me the place always looked and stank like a garbage dump—but I'd never thought it was this bad, that they had to sleep on the floor.

The room was full of all these big candles, the scented kind. There must have been forty or fifty of them. And big melted patches where there must have been lots more, but they'd burned down and been replaced. There was a box full of them by the dresser, all ready to go. They also had a couple of those weird-looking incense burners going. It made me want to laugh. There were more different smells in that room than I'd smelled my whole life. And all of them so sweet they made my eyes water.

But under the sweet there was something else—when a breeze sneaked through and flickered the candles I thought I could smell it—like when we got back from vacation that summer and the freezer broke down while we were away. Mom made Dad move us to a motel for a while. Something like that, but it was having a hard time digging itself out of all that sweetness.

"Candles cost a fortune," Jesse said. "All the money in my dad's wallet plus the coins my mom kept in a fruit jar. She didn't even think I knew about that. But they look pretty neat, huh?"

I took a step into the room and looked at his dad's mouth. Then his mom's mouth. They hung open like they were about to swallow a fly or sing or something. I almost laughed again, but I couldn't. Their mouths looked a little like my dad's mouth, the way he lets it hang open when he falls asleep on the couch watching TV. But different. Their mouths were soft and loose, their lips dark, all dry and cracked, but even though they were holding their mouths open so long no saliva came dripping out. And there was gray and blue under their eyes. There were dark blotches on Jesse's mom's face. They were so still, like they were playing a game on me. Without even thinking about it I pushed on his dad's leg with my foot. It was like pushing against a board. His dad rocked a little, but he was so tight his big arms didn't even wiggle. Jesse always said his old man was “too tight.” I really did start to laugh, thinking about that, but it was like my breath exploded instead. I didn’t even know I had been holding it. “Jesus…” I could feel my chest shake all by itself.

Jesse looked at me almost like he was surprised, like I’d done something wrong. “I told you, didn’t I? Don’t be a baby.” He sat down on the floor and started playing with his dad’s leg, pushing on it and trying to lift up the knee. “Last night they both started getting stiff. It really happens, you know? It’s not just something in the movies. You know why it happens, John?” He looked up at me, but he was still poking the leg with his fist, like he was trying to make his dad do something, slap him or something. Any second I figured his dad would reach over and grab Jesse by the hair and pull him down onto the floor beside them.

I shook my head. I was thinking no no no, but I couldn’t quite get that out.

Jesse hit his dad on the thigh hard as he could. It sounded like an overstuffed leather chair. It didn’t give at all. “Hell, I don’t know either. Maybe it’s the body fighting off being dead, even after you’re dead, you know? It gets all mad and stiff on you.” He laughed but it didn’t sound much like Jesse’s laugh. “I guess it don’t know it’s dead. It don’t know shit once the brain is dead. But if I was going to die I guess I’d fight real hard.” Jesse looked at his mom and dad and made a twisted face like he was smelling them for the first time. “Bunch of pussies ...”

He grabbed the arm his dad had folded against his chest and tried to pull it away. His dad held on but then the arm bent a little. The fat shoulders shook when Jesse let go and his dad fell back. The head hit the pillow and left a greasy red smear.

“The old man here started loosening up top a few hours ago, in the same order he got stiff in.” Jesse reached over and pinched his dad’s left cheek.

“Christ, Jesse!” I ran back into the hall and fell on the floor. I could hardly breathe. Then I started crying, really bawling, and I could breathe again.

After awhile I could feel Jesse patting me on the back. "You never saw dead people before, huh, Johnny?"

I just shook my head. "I'm s-sorry, Jesse. I'm s-so sorry."

"They were old," he said. "It's okay. Really."

I looked up at him. I didn't understand. It felt like he wasn't even speaking English. But he just looked at me, then looked back into his parents' bedroom, and didn't say anything more. Finally, I knew I had to say something. "How did it happen?"

He looked at me like I was being the one hard to understand. "I told you. They were old."

I thought about the red smear his dad's head made on the pillow, but I couldn't get myself to understand it. "But, Jesse... at the same time?"

He shook his head. "What's wrong with you, John? My dad died first. I guess that made my mom so sad she died a few minutes later. You've heard of that. First one old person dies, then the person they're married to dies just a short time after?"

"Yeah..."

"Their hearts just stopped beating." I looked up at him. I could feel my own heart vibrating in my chest, so hard it hurt my ribs. "I put them together like that. They were my parents. I figured they'd like that."

He had that right, I guess. After all, they were his parents. Maybe he didn't always get along with them, but they were his parents. He could look at them after they were dead.

I made myself look at them. It was a lot easier the second time. A whole lot easier. I felt a little funny about that. Even without his dad's blood on the pillow they were a lot different from sleeping people. There was just no movement at all, and hardly any color but the blue, and they both looked cool, but not a damp kind of cool because they looked so dry, and their eyelids weren't shut all the way, and you could see a little sliver of white where the lids weren't all the way closed. I made myself get as close to their eyes as I could, maybe to make sure one final time they weren't pretending. The sliver of white was dull, like on a fish. Like something thick and milky had grown over their eyes. They looked like dummies some department store had thrown out in the garbage. There wasn't anything alive about them at all.

"When did they die?"

Jesse was looking at them, too. Closely, like they were the strangest things anyone had ever seen. "It's been at least a day, I guess. Almost two."

Jesse said we shouldn't call the police just yet. They were his parents, weren't they? Didn't he have the right to be with them for awhile? I couldn't argue with that. I guessed Jesse had all kinds of rights when it was his parents. But it still felt weird, him being with their dead bodies almost two whole days. I helped him light some more candles when he said the air wasn't sweet enough anymore. I felt a little better helping him do that, like we were having a funeral for them. All those sweet-smelling candles and incense felt real religious. Then I felt bad about thinking he was being weird earlier, like I was being prejudiced or something. But it was there just the same. I quit looking at his mom and dad, except when Jesse told me to. And after a couple of hours of me just standing out in the hallway, or fussing with the candles, trying not to look at them, Jesse started insisting.

"You gotta look at them, John."

"I did. You saw me. I looked at them."

"No, I mean really look at them. You haven't seen everything there is to see."

I looked at him instead. Real hard. I could hardly believe he was saying this. "Why? I'm sorry they're dead. But why do I have to look at them?"

"Because I want you to."

"Jesse…"

"… and besides, you should know about these things. Your mom and dad don't want you to know about things like this but I guess it's about the most important thing to know about there is. Everybody gets scared of dying, and just about everybody is scared of the dead. You remember that movie Zombie we rented? That's what it was all about. Now we've got two dead bodies here. You're my friend, and I want to help you out. I want to share something with you."

"Christ, Jesse. They're your parents."

"What, you think I don't know that? Who else should I learn about this stuff from anyway? If they were still alive, they'd be supposed to teach me. What's wrong with it? And don't just tell me because it's 'weird.' People say something's weird because it makes them nervous. Just because it bothers them they don't want you to do it. So what do we care, anyway? Nobody else is gonna know about this."

Jesse could argue better than anybody, and I never knew what to think about anything for sure. Before I knew it he had me back in the bedroom, leaning over the bodies. It was a little better—I guess I was getting used to them. At least I didn't feel ready to throw up like I did a while ago. That surprised me. It surprised me even more when he took my hand and put it on his mom's—his dead mom's—arm, and I didn't jerk it away.

"Jesus . . ." I guess I'd expected it to be still stiff, but it had gotten soft again, as soft as anything I'd ever felt, like I could just dig my fingers into her arm like butter. It was cool, but not what I expected. And dry.

"See the spots?" Jesse said behind me. "Like somebody's been painting her. Like for one of those freak shows. Oh, she'd hate it if she knew. She'd think she looked like a whore!"

I saw them all right. Patches of blue-green low down on his dad's belly. Before I could stop him he raised his mom's skirt and showed me that the marks on her were worse: more of the blue-green and little patches of greenish red, all of it swimming together around her big white panties. I was embarrassed, but I kept staring. That's the way I'd always imagined seeing my first panties on a woman: when she was asleep or—to tell the truth—when she was dead. I used to dream about dead women in their panties and bras, dead women naked with their parts hanging out, and I'd felt ashamed about it, but here it was happening for the real and for some reason

I was having a hard time feeling too ashamed. I hadn't done it; I hadn't killed her.

"Look," he said. I followed his hand as it moved up his mother's belly. I tensed as he pulled her dress up further, back over her head so that I couldn't see her mouth anymore, her mouth hanging open like she was screaming, but no sound coming out. "I know you always wanted to see one of these up close. Admit it, John." His hand rested on the right cup of her bra. Now I felt real bad, and ashamed, like I had helped him kill her. Her white, loose skin spilled out of the top and bottom of the cup like big gobs of dough. With a jerk of his hand Jesse pulled his mother's bra off. The skin was loose and it all had swollen so much it was beginning to tear. I knew it was going to break like an old fruit any second. "She's gotten bigger since the thing happened," he said. I started to choke. "Come on, John. You always wanted to see this stuff. You wanted to see it, and you wanted to see it dead."

I turned away and walked back into the hall when he started to laugh. His mom was an it now. His dad was a thing. But Jesse knew me so well. He knew about the dreams and he knew what would get to me, what I always thought about, even though I'd never told him. It made me wonder if all guys my age think about being dead that way, wanting to see it and touch it, wanting something real like that, even though it was so awful. I used to dream about finding my own parents dead, and what they would look like, but never once did I imagine I would do that to them. Not like Jesse. I knew now what Jesse had done to his parents. No question about that anymore. But I was all mixed up about what I felt about it. Because, even though it was awful, I still wanted to look, and touch. Wasn't that almost as bad?

"Here." Jesse grabbed my arm and turned me around. He led me back over to his mother's body. "You don't have to look. You can close your eyes. Let me just take your hand." But I wanted to look. He took me over to her side. There was a big blister there, full of stuff. Jesse put my hand on it. "Feel weird, huh?" He didn't look crazy; he looked like some kind of young scientist or something from some dumb TV show. I nodded. "Hey, look at her mouth!" I did. In her big loose mouth I could see pieces of food that had come up. A little dark bug crawled up out of her hair. This is what it's like, what it's really like, I thought. I thought about those rock stars I used to like all made up like they were dead, those horror movies I used to watch with Jesse, and all those stoner kids I used to know getting high every chance they had and telling me it don't matter anyway and everything was just a drag with their eyes half shut and their mouths hanging open and their skin getting whiter every day. All of them, they don't know shit about it, I thought. This is what it's really like.

Jesse left me by his mom and started going to the candles one at a time, snuffing them out. A filmy gray smoke started to fill the bedroom. I could already smell the mix of sweet and sharp smells starting to go away, and underneath that the other truly awful smell creeping in.

Jesse turned to me while the last few candles were still lit. That bad smell was almost all over me now, but I just sat there, holding my breath and waiting for it. He almost grinned but didn't guite make it. "I guess you're ready to take a hit off all this now," he said. I just stared at him. And then I let my clean breath go.

And now Jesse says he figures it's about time we did another one.

We took off from his house with the one bike and Jesse's pack but we had to walk most of the time because Jesse figured we'd better go cross-country, over the fences and through the trees where nobody could see us. He didn't think they'd find the bodies anytime soon but my parents would report me missing after awhile. It was hell getting the bike through all that stuff but Jesse said we might need it later so we best take it. The scariest part was when we had to cross a couple of creeks, and wading through water up over my belt carrying that bike made me sure I was going to drown. But I thought maybe I even deserved it for what I'd seen, what I'd done, and what I didn't do. I thought about what a body must look like after it drowned—I'd heard they swole up something awful, and I thought about Jesse showing off my body after I'd died, letting people poke it and smell it, and then I didn't want to die anymore.

Once Jesse suggested that maybe we should build a raft and float downriver like Tom Sawyer and Huckleberry Finn. I'd read the two books and he'd seen one of the movies. I thought it was a great idea but then we couldn't figure out how to do it. Jesse bitched about how they don't teach you important stuff like that in school, and used to, dads taught you stuff like raft-building but they didn't anymore. He said his dad should have taught him stuff like that but he was always too busy.

"Probably," I said, watching Jesse closer all the time because he seemed to be getting frustrated with everything.

I thought a lot about Tom and Huck that first day and how they came back into town just in time to see their own funeral. I wondered if every kid dreamed about doing that. I wondered if my parents found out about what I did in Jesse's house what they would say about me at my funeral.

We slept the first night under the trees. Or tried to. Jesse walked around a lot in the dark and I couldn't sleep much from watching him. The next morning he was nervous and agitated and first thing he did he found an old dog and beat it over the head with a hammer. I didn't know he had the hammer but it was in his pack and I pretty much guessed what he'd used it for before. He didn't even tell me he was going to do it, he just saw the dog and as soon as he saw it he did it. We both stood there and looked at the body and touched it and kicked it and I didn't feel a damn thing and I don't think Jesse did either because he was still real nervous.

Later that morning the farmer picked us up in his truck.

"Going far?" he asked us from the window and I wanted to tell him to keep driving mister but I didn't. He was old and had a nice face and was probably somebody's father and some kid's grandfather but I couldn't say a thing with Jesse standing there.

"Meadville," Jesse said, smiling. I'd seen that fakey smile on Jesse's face before, when he talked to adults, when he talked to his own parents. "We're gonna help out on my uncle's farm." Jesse smiled and smiled and my throat and my chest and my head started filling up with that awful smell again. The old man looked at me and all I could do was look at him and nod. He let Jesse into the cab of the truck and told me I'd better ride with my bike in the back. The old man smiled at me a real smile, like I was a good boy.

The breeze was cool in the back of the truck and the bed rocked so on the gravelly side road we were on I started falling asleep, but every time I was getting ready to conk out we'd hit a bump or something and my head would snap up. But I still think I must have slept a little because somewhere in there I started to dream. I dreamed that I was riding along in the back of a pickup truck my grandfather was driving. He'd been singing the whole way and I'd been enjoying his singing but then it wasn't singing anymore it was screaming and a monster was in the front seat with him, Death was in the front seat with him, beating him over the head with a hammer. Then the truck jerked to a stop and I looked through the cab window where Death was hammering the brains out of my grandfather and coating the glass with gray and brown and red. My grandfather scratched at the glass like I should do something but I couldn't because it was just a dream. Then Death turned to me and grinned while he was still swinging the hammer and fighting with my grandfather and it was my face grinning and speckled with brains and blood.

I turned around to try to get out of the dream, to watch the trees whizz by while the truck was rocking me to sleep, but the land was dark and the trees were tall bodies all swollen in their dying and their heavy heads hanging down and their loose mouths falling open. And the wind through the trees was the breath of the dead—that awful smell I thought we'd left back at Jesse's house.

Later I kissed my grandfather goodbye and helped Jesse bury him under one of those tall trees that smelled so bad.

And now Jesse says he figures it's about time we did another one. He grins and says he's lost the smell. But I can smell it all the time—I smell, taste, and breathe that smell.

Outside Meadville, Jesse washed up and stole a shirt and pants off a clothesline. From there we took turns walking and riding the bike to a mall where Jesse did some panhandling. We used the money to buy shakes and burgers. While we were eating, Jesse said that panhandling wasn't wrong if you had to do it to get something to eat. I couldn't watch Jesse eat—the food kept coming up out of his mouth. My two burgers smelled so bad I tried to hold my breath while I ate them but that made me choke. But I still ate them. I was hungry.

We walked around the mall for a long time. Other people did the same thing, staring, but never buying anything. It reminded me of one of those zombie pictures. I tried not to touch anybody because they smelled so bad and they held their mouths open so that you could see all their teeth.

Finally, Jesse picked out two girls and dragged me over to them. I couldn't get too close because of their smell, but the younger one seemed to like me. She had a nice smile. I looked at Jesse's face. He was grinning at them and then at me. His complexion had gotten real bad since we'd started travelling—there'd been more and more zits on his face every day. Now they were huge. One burst open and a long skinny white worm crawled out. I looked at the girls—they didn't seem to notice.

"His parents are putting him up for adoption so we ran away. I'm trying to hide him until they change their minds." Jesse's breath stank.

The girls looked at me. "Really?" the older one said. Her face had tiny cracks in it. I looked down at my feet.

Both of the girls said "I'm sorry" about the same time, then they got quiet like they were embarrassed. But I still didn't look up. I watched their sandaled feet and the black bugs crawling between their toes.

The older one could drive, so they hid us in the back seat of their car and drove to the end of the drive that led to the farmhouse where their family lived. We were supposed to go on to the barn and the girls would bring us out some food later. We never told them about my bike and I kept thinking about it and what people would say when they found it. Even though I never used the bike anymore I was a little sorry about having lost it.

I also thought about those girls and how nice they were and how the younger one seemed to like me, even though they smelled so bad. I wondered why girls like that were always so nice to guys like us, guys with a story to tell, and I thought about how dumb it was.

After we were in the barn for a couple of hours, the girls—they were sisters, if I didn't mention it before—brought us some food. The younger one talked to me a long time while I ate but I don't remember anything she said. The older one talked to Jesse the same way and I heard her say, "You're a good person to be helping your friend like this." She leaned over and kissed Jesse on his cheek even though the zits were tearing his face apart. Her shirt rode up on the side and Jesse put his dirty hand there. I saw the blisters rise up out of her skin and break open and the smell was worse than ever in the barn but no one else seemed to notice.

I finished eating and leaned back into the dirty straw. I liked the younger sister but I hoped she wouldn't kiss me the same way. I couldn't stand the idea of her open, loose mouth touching my skin. Underneath the straw I saw that there were hunks of gray flesh, pieces of arms and legs and things inside you I didn't know the name for. But I covered them over with more straw when nobody was looking, and I didn't say anything.

And now Jesse says he figures it's about time we did another one. He thinks I've forgotten. But I haven't.

I've been thinking about the two sisters all night and how much they trust us and how good they've been to us. And

I've been thinking how they remind me of the Wilks sisters in Huckleberry Finn and how Huck felt so ornery and low down because he was letting the duke and king rob them of their money after the sisters had been so nice to him. Sometimes I guess you don't know how to behave until you've read it in a book or seen it on TV.

So he gets up from his nest in the sour straw and starts toward the barn door. And I get up out of the straw and follow. Only last night I took the hammer, and now I beat him in the head until his head comes apart, and all the stink comes out and covers me so bad I know I'll never get it off. He always said he'd fight really hard if he knew he was dying, but his body doesn't fight back hardly at all. Maybe he didn't know.

I hear the noises in the farmhouse and now there are voices and flashlights coming. I scrape my fingers through the straw to find all the pieces of Jesse's head to make him look a little better for these people. I lie down in the straw beside him and close my eyes, leaving just a sliver of milky white under each lid to show them. I drop my mouth open and stop my saliva. I imagine the blue-green colors that will come and paint my body. I imagine the blisters and the insects and the terrible smell my breath has become. But mostly I try to imagine how I'm going to explain to these strangers why I'm enjoying this.

STONES

Sometimes when he looked at his hands, he could see them hardening, the skin flaking away, the muscles stiffening, and suddenly he was earth again, suddenly he was stone.

Every few months when Carter first felt the weakness, he would make a trip to the place of the stones. Here, he would stare at the rounded boulders, the broken fragments, the huge dark slabs pushed out of the sandy soil, until the weakness passed. The weakness, which came upon him fiercely, usually manifested itself as an overwhelming need to die. This seemed reasonable. The whole world was dying around him. Cities deteriorated, falling into rubble. Streams slowed down from all the garbage they contained. People in general seemed more sluggish than he remembered from childhood. It was as if everything he saw was slowly solidifying, losing energy, turning to stone. As if this were the natural state of things. And so the weakness came, a compulsion to be turned into stone.

When the weakness passed, Carter would leave the stones, go out and take someone else's life away from them. Freeze their existence. Turn them into stone instead.

The stones always made him feel better.

The stones lay scattered across a high hilltop five miles from the small house where Carter grew up. He'd asked about them in town—one old man who used to be a schoolteacher said they had been deposited there by glacier action. But Carter could not believe the stones could be that old.

There were three or four stones the size of boulders, probably several tons apiece. He imagined they must have come from some place deep underground, where everything was larger than life. These were rounded, with only slight depressions. A half-dozen stones one step down in size were much more angular, with many sharp edges, as if they had broken off larger stones. The scale of stones went down from there. To smaller rounded pieces that still might crush a body completely if dropped a distance. To large rocks for pounding a skull in. To fragments sharp and dangerous as ancient arrowheads. Down to water-smooth pebbles ready for a slingshot, the size of harsh thoughts worn from repetition.

Every time Carter came here, he would stare at the stones for hours, seeking some sort of summation which would keep them solid in his mind forever. But stones were hard to define. Loose estimations of size, looser descriptions of shape.

All stones, he theorized, had come down from the original stone, the huge mass that had given birth to everything by destroying itself. All glory, all life came from this unreasoning, dead stone. After thrashing about in cold silence, it had awakened from its long dream as a world, lived on by these parasitic creatures called human beings.

The history of this original stone, as with all stones, must have been a history of splittings and fallings apart: slab became boulder and boulder became stone and stone became pebbles rolled and smoothed by the outer lips of an enormous sea.

Carter played close attention to how soil filled the cracks in the stone, plants growing where once it had been impervious. This, he concluded, was how life first began in the midst of cold, hard death.

The remainders of this great original stone, the slabs and peaks of it, became the distant mountains, and were used to build the temples of human beings.

Stone constantly reminds us of our own deaths, he thought.

Watching the pebbles gathered about the bases of the larger stones, trailing off into grass and dirt, always filled Carter with a nameless anxiety. Separate from its larger pieces, stone drifts, wanders, moved by people and scattered by the wind. The center does not hold. Anywhere.

The stones were unyielding, blind, and despite their constant exposure to all weathers, always dry.

Each time he came here, he walked slowly up the hill, his chest gradually filling with stones. A fresh body in his arms. Sometimes the skin of the body would be bruised, if his knife had not been efficient enough, and he'd had to use a stone to remind the flesh of both its origins and its destiny. Sometimes he might try to press a stone into the victim's head, pounding until the skull broke and the stone lodged there like a jewel. The pieces of skull themselves were like poor cousins to stone, a reminder of how far human beings had declined in their devolution.

Over the years his eyes had hardened, gone to stone. His tongue had the stillness of stone. But, of course, the world was stone, and more and more he felt a part of it.

He would lay the body down among the larger stones, then pick up a fist-sized piece, the size and shape of a brain. Holding the stone in his hand was like holding the world.

He thought to tell the stones about the dreams and aspirations, the life history of his latest victim, but the language of the stones had no words for such things. Instead he would stoop and fill his victim's mouth with the pebbles he found.

The stones grew harder the longer he looked. They thrived on the intensity of his gaze. He would touch them worshipfully. Touching stone, his fingers imitated its stiffness, its need to be all in one place.

Each time he would bend down to kiss his victims, but their mouths would be filled with stone.

Sometimes, if he stared long enough, he found he could climb inside the stones, despite their increased hardness.

Inside the stones it was quiet. Inside the stones he could lie down and watch the pictures moving slowly across their inner walls.

There were always pictures of children, and lovers he would never have, and more victims he would desperately try to bring closer with his knife. Sometimes he regretted loving his victims so much that he had to kill them, although he wasn't sure where such guilt came from.

All flesh was stone in any case, only in its initial soft phase. And everyone knew it was impossible to kill a stone.

UGLY BEHAVIOR

"Sing motherfuckin' 'Ugly Behavior'! Sing motherfuckin' 'Ugly Behavior'!" The crowd was screaming it now, but JK didn't care. Let them scream their lungs out. It was his show, and the crowd could hate him as much as he hated them, he didn't care. He decided when he sang what, when he did what, walk off the stage or give them the sickest show they'd ever seen, the real show. He got to decide. It was the first thing in his life he could say that about.

Hard to tell how many of them were out there. The lights were up too bright. He couldn't see much more than pieces of faces past the front row, but there was definitely some young stuff out there. Like that one, the blonde, how the fuck old was she? She looked like a baby.

When JK glanced down at his arms and legs, he thought he looked like an over-exposed black-and-white photograph. The scars on his arms were like ink lines. He danced and pranced, wishing for a strobe light.

Back behind him, Dean worked on a sloppy drum roll. His drumming got worse every week, not that it mattered much. JK had told him more than once to cut out the stupid drum rolls—they sounded like Dean was making fun of him, though JK wasn't clear exactly how. Maybe tomorrow night he'd pull

Dean off his drum kit and kick his ass. He'd fuck him up good. The crowd would love that. Jack and Lee wouldn't interfere—it was about all they could do to hold onto their guitars.

The place smelled like shit, but that was a good thing. Made JK feel right at home, knee deep in the shit and ugly.

"There's just no call for all that ugly behavior," was what JK's grandma always said. But JK's grandma didn't understand rock and roll. JK had made his living for ten years behaving ugly, and though it had been mostly small-time gigs, cassettes and then CDs from small, independent labels, a few paintings sold to hardcore fans, it had been good enough. Some years about half of it went up his nose, but that was okay. Business expense. Nobody ever said being an artist was the easy way.

Oh, there was plenty of "call" for it, all right. All JK had to do was look at tonight's crowd, beggin' for 'Ugly Behavior'. But he never argued the point with her. A woman of her generation wasn't supposed to understand—that was part of it and always had been. Not doing what they told you to do and stickin' it up their asses and speaking to your own generation, although most of JK's fans were a lot younger, with a sprinkling of guys his age who he seriously doubted were true fans—not that any of that crap mattered—but who were mostly into it for the opportunity at underage pussy.

Not that they'd get much—bunch of fat pricks in glasses wearing black JK T-shirts too tight across the belly. Tonight they were the ones pushing up to the front of the stage, their damn glasses shiny like bottles, blinding him under these bright lights. What the hell did they know about kicking open the doors of perception?

No real loyalty there, or anywhere, for that matter. Every fan JK ever met was a liar. "JK, you're the shit!" the guy in the green T-shirt spat, eyes rolling off the top of his head.

"JK, you say the truth like nobody can!" some fat chick whined.

And "JK, we love you man!" Somebody always said that,

a few dozen times a night. He hated these cock suckers. But what was he going to do? They kept him in beer and drugs.

"You suck!" A guy after his own heart. But even that guy, did he really think JK sucked, or was he just saying it to entertain his buddies?

And there was that blonde. Fuck! She was just a kid—this was no place for kids! Where were her fuckin' parents?

JK didn't always get along with his old granny, but she'd been the only one he could trust to say what she really felt. She'd raised him when his mom ran off at sixteen, seventeen whatever that scum bag whore. He did owe his mom one thing, though, the knowledge that you got nothing left to lose which every artist needs if he's going to do real work and not just what's safe and profitable. It was like in 'Ugly Behavior,' when he yelled "If you gonna be real you gotta do something ugly!" and he sang that line about ten or twelve times in a row, depending on how he was feeling that night, and the crowd yelled it right along with him, until at the end he pulled out his dick and started pissing on the stage, or if he was already hard by then he might jack off onto the front row, and by that time the crowd was going crazy, yelling and screaming, because, of course, that's why they came in the first place.

Each night he did something a little different with 'Ugly Behavior,' something spontaneous based on his reading of the crowd. Tonight he was already well into the show and he hadn't decided yet what he was going to do.

The really creative part was choosing the ugly thing he was going to do in that last minute or two, and that's what was so great about live performance. It took a lot of self-discipline, though, to get it all timed out right, and still stay spontaneous. Any jackass could masturbate on stage—it took an artist to know when to come.

He looked around for the kid, didn't see her. Maybe her parents got some sense finally, got her outta there. Motherfuckers trying to save on babysitters. Motherfuckin' scum.

Inspired, JK started into 'Scum Bag Whore,' his mouth

stretched as wide as he could make it. He stuck the black ball of the microphone in as far as he could, practically swallowing it, making a gargling noise after every "scum." One night he had almost swallowed it, running across the stage with it in his mouth, tripping on a cord. It had made him gag, and he'd thrown up on stage. Everybody'd thought it was part of the show. Stupid fuckers. He hadn't been able to sing for a week after that.

The stupid pricks in front kept yelling for 'Ugly Behavior,' louder and louder until you couldn't hear 'Scum Bag Whore,' you pretty much couldn't hear anything but them. He cleared his throat and hawked a loogey in their direction but the motherfuckers just laughed.

The main thing was, he had to hold off doing 'Ugly Behavior' until at least near the end of his first set. Most places there wasn't going to be a second set because either the fans got too rowdy or JK got too rowdy, somebody got hurt, somebody got offended, somebody got stabbed, the police were called, or the management chickened out even though they all knew what JK did before they hired him, hell, wasn't that why they'd hired him? It was all a bunch of happy horse shit.

He started singing the opening to 'My Prick Wears A Necklace,' the serious part, where he's singing about the diagnosis, got about ten lines in, when somebody threw a bottle up on stage. He picked it up, started to throw it back into the crowd, but stopped himself. If he did that they'd shut the show down for sure, and he didn't like leaving the stage without singing 'Ugly Behavior' first. And the time wasn't quite right.

If JK didn't wait for the right time to sing 'Ugly Behavior,' if he gave in to all those fuckers who'd been yelling at him since the opening number "Sing motherfuckin' 'Ugly Behavior'!" then they'd be getting what they paid for too early and they wouldn't much want to listen while he finished his set they'd just want him to do something new, something worse and sometimes things just got out of hand, or more out of hand than they were supposed to.

That was pretty much what went wrong that time outside Memphis at the Headlights Roadhouse. He'd been swallowing everything anybody gave him that day, all kinds of pretty pills and sweet liquors, and he did a couple of lines before going on stage, and then they were handing him beers on stage which for the most part he spat back out at them but he drank a lot of it, too.

Then they started in on that 'Ugly Behavior' shit, that chanting "We want 'Ugly Behavior'!" shit halfway into the first song, 'Ice Pick In The Head.' It was pissing him off because they weren't listening. A bunch of drunk college guys down in front were the ones that started it—they'd brought dates. He'd seen it before—the guy brings a girl promising her a freak show which JK could pretty much be counted on to deliver. Well, let the motherfucker feel superior, as long as he paid for two tickets.

It must have been the combination of everything he'd taken that day, plus the hot lights and just the natural agitation that came with performing. Suddenly JK felt warm and wet in the crotch. He wasn't sure what it was at first—you felt all kinds of sensations on stage—it wasn't unusual for JK to perform with a hard-on, or with his clothes sweated through, or with his body reeking of spilt beer or jack d. Then he smelled it—JK had just pissed himself. It wasn't intentional, and that was what bothered him—it would have been okay if it had been part of the act. It being unintentional made him feel like some pissy old man.

About the same time he noticed it the guys up front started hooting and their pretty dates looked embarrassed. He started to feel like he was losing the edge—there was a fine line between offending people and just embarrassing yourself. One was rock and roll and the other was riding the short bus. He had to do something to take control again so he just sat down on the stage, kicked off his shoes and stripped off his pants and boxers. That wound up the crowd pretty good. He paraded up and down the stage just wearing his T-shirt, then he thought what-the-hell and tore that off, too, threw it into that crowd of assholes. Then he pranced up to the front edge of the stage and wiggled his dick.

He'd pulled his dick out before on stage to relieve himself or whatever. And he'd been a little self-conscious the first few times. It wasn't like he had a rock star pecker; if anything it was of less than ordinary size. A lot of jokers pointed and laughed, but JK didn't give a shit. Being monster stoned helped. After the first couple of times he'd trimmed the pubic hair back from the base of his dick because that made it look bigger. But he knew it still wasn't anything to brag about. But that was part of the point, wasn't it?

So there he was dancing around naked and wiggling his junk for the amusement of the crowd. The band was laughing, playing nothing in particular, just jamming with themselves. He sang a few more lines of 'Ice Pick' but he'd lost his place in the song. So he sang a lot more chorus: "Ice pick! Ice pick! Ice pick in the head! Ice pick! Ice pick! Poke me 'til I'm dead!" He made up a verse that wasn't too bad—if he could remember it later he'd write it down. But experience had taught him he probably wouldn't. He was pretty sure the gig was going to end soon. He fully expected to be pulled off the stage any second, for the management to shut them down or the cops to arrive. But that didn't happen, at least not right away, and he didn't know if that was because the club was making some good money or if whoever was in charge was just asleep at the wheel. Not that it mattered much; it gave him a lot more time than usual to do his thing. But just to make sure, he didn't break for the second set; he and the band kept right on playing.

The problem was he was still prancing around naked, and he hadn't yet done the whole 'Ugly Behavior' routine, and he didn't know where else he could go with it. About fifteen minutes into what should have been their second set, the crowd looked bored. There were still scattered insults, things thrown up on the stage, but JK could tell their hearts weren't really in it.

He figured he'd just jack off onto the front row and call it a day, so he started pumping what little bit of wrinkled pud he had, but as much as he played with it and slapped at it, he couldn't get his prick hard.

Just to buy himself some extra time to think of something else, he picked up a broken sliver of beer bottle and started cutting on his arms and chest, taking his time to place each mark, applying as much artistic consideration as possible, using the fingers of his left hand to smear the blood, and though that sparked a little excitement, the crowd was soon spending more time talking to each other than watching the show. Rock and roll was supposed to be like a good train wreck—you shouldn't be able to pull your eyes away.

And JK wasn't feeling it, either. He was pretty much dragging. He'd been thinking about how they were booked for three hours, and the band didn't have three hours worth of material. They'd never needed it before—somebody always stopped the show before the end of hour two.

JK kept thinking I don't need this shit I don't need this shit and that's, really, what gave him the idea. His artistic inspiration. Creative people think that way—they trust the notion, they run with the spur of the moment. JK turned his back on the audience, squatted, and shit on the stage. Then he twirled back around in this crazy prehistoric ballet move, scooped up the runny shit and threw it on those fuckers in the front row.

It was pretty gratifying the way things went to hell after that, the cops coming in, at long fucking last, and it became pretty much a riot with those trying to tear JK a new asshole and those wanting the concert to keep going. Chairs and bottles were flying and people were jumping around trying to keep, literally, out of the shit. Bunch of people got bloodied, thoroughly getting their money's worth. JK and the band snuck out under cover of the confusion. They didn't get paid but JK kept telling the band it was a valuable contribution toward their artistic evolution.

Word got back to Granny when some local reporter wanted to "ask you about that incident in Tennessee." She phoned JK up and gave him another long talk about that "ugly behavior" and then wouldn't speak to him for several months. It wasn't her fault, she just didn't understand rock and roll. Rock and roll was all about doing what you weren't supposed to do. Rock and roll was vile and offensive and breaking the wall and breaking the law. JK felt pretty bad about her not talking to him—whatever their differences, she was all he had—but he didn't hold it against her. She'd been the only one to ever give a damn and he owed her. People as a whole he'd pretty much take or leave but mostly leave with a kick in the head for good measure. Granny was the only one he'd ever felt any kind of love for. Sure, he'd robbed her a couple of times, but that was just for drug money, nothing personal, he couldn't have helped that.

Memphis changed everything, got them into the papers and on the news and that set the pattern for every show after that. The fellow in the local paper—a total asshole—called it the beginning of JK's long decline. As far as JK was concerned, he had found himself and his artistic mission all in one night. JK got interviewed a lot after that, and every time one of those fuckers complained, he told them they didn't understand rock and roll.

The problem with the shows was that topping himself each time became harder and harder to do.

JK drug out "My Prick Wears A Necklace" as long as he could, pulling his prick out and singing to it, running his finger around the head until it became angry and red and too irritated to touch. Something about the intensity of that quieted the crowd down some, got them to buy more drinks, which had to please the club management. This song was the closest thing the band had to a ballad—it was the pause before the storm, the songs after this building in volume and ridiculousness until they hit 'Ugly Behavior.'

JK was getting cold, so he did something he'd never done on stage before—he put some clothes back on. Earlier in the evening some skinny girl had taken off her slacks and top and thrown them up on stage, danced around in just her bra and panties, then disappeared. Their two roadies, Wilt and Leon, had used her clothes to wipe up some of the piss and beer to reduce the chance of JK falling and busting his head open (Not that it would be the worst thing to happen—if done correctly it could add to a performance), so the pants were too small, and really rank, but he squeezed himself into them anyway.

Those tight girly pants made JK feel just like a ballet dancer in tights, all light and frisky, and that inspired him to jump around and kick up his legs. The crowd hooted and cheered, and that boosted the energy level as he launched into 'Kill the Bitch!' Guys got off on that song because it talked about "Every woman ever denied you, criticized you, left you hated, made you castrated," listed every way possible a woman could make you feel bad, ending up with that three-word chorus, "Kill the bitch!" sung by most of the guys in the room and some of the women, and JK liked kicking up his heels on that one, which worked pretty well in too-tight pants. They ripped a little, showing off his balls, but yes ma'am that's showbiz for you. JK picked a woman in the front row to sing the chorus to, just like he always did, and that pissed off the guy with her: some tall blond frat guy in a yellow sweater, but the kid oughta expect that, going to a JK show. Trying to protect your girl, well, hell, how out-of-touch was that? At least JK didn't spit in her face, which he'd been known to do.

'Kill the Bitch!' did its job, getting the crowd worked up, and giving JK a head full of steam into 'Ice Pick In The Head!' which he'd moved later in the show after that performance outside Memphis. It had become a lot more popular with the crowds since then, become a kind of anthem for poor fuckers everywhere who'd reached that point where nothing works any more to make them feel better: not philosophy, not booze, not drugs, not sex, hell, not even rock and roll. Because people get that way. They just get to the point where nothing takes them where they need to go. And that's the pain of living in this world.

"Ice pick in the head! Ice pick in the head!" JK screamed it, making a stabbing motion with his closed right fist, bringing it closer to his head until finally he was pounding himself in the ear again and again, beating his head until it hurt, until it was harder to hear the crowd screaming, until it was harder to hear his own screaming. "That's what I need!" he screamed. "Ice pick in the head!"

A lot of these kids probably didn't even know what an ice pick was, what with their built-in ice makers and ice shavers, that yuppie shit their parents all bought, unless they'd seen an ice pick in a horror flick one time, used as a murder weapon. But the pounding, trying to beat some idea into your head, they'd understand that, he figured. That shit was universal.

But JK, he still wanted to stick with using that phrase "ice pick." Because that's what this song was meant to be. A murder weapon.

And that was pretty much all JK remembered of the show the next morning. He would have gone into 'Ugly Behavior' after that, the energy would have been high, the crowd would have been shouting the chorus along with him, egging him on, then he would have done something truly outrageous, something his sweet old granny wouldn't want to know about.

In other words, more of the usual. He really didn't need to remember the specifics. Same old same old. And waking up the next morning feeling like he'd gotten nowhere.

Except this wasn't his usual nowhere. He was lying on something hard and cold. Stinking. It wouldn't be the first time he woke up on some toilet floor, but that wasn't it, no. The side of his face was stuck hard to the floor. He tried to grin, but couldn't. It wouldn't be the first time he passed out in his food, but it would be a first time for pancake syrup. He loved his syrup, especially when his grandma made those big, fluffy, handmade pancakes. Granny always said he used way too much syrup. Drowning in it. "You must not like my pancakes," she always said, "you drown them in sweet syrup like that!" But he loved them, oh, he loved them. Just like he loved her. So she didn't understand rock and roll. Well, he didn't understand much else.

But all this syrup, this strawberry maple syrup, drowning in it, wasn't syrup, was it? He felt the knowledge of it, in his head, like an . . . ice pick. No, not syrup at all.

He was in an alley. He could see the cans, the filthy cardboard boxes. He could smell the exhaust. The piss and shit stink. Directly in front of him was a wall of dark, scummy brick. And that little blonde girl, that beautiful little girl, sitting there where no little girl should be.

What the fuck? He tried to speak, but all he could do was whisper. "Go away," he said. "You don't want to see this." But she said nothing. She just stared.

Sun glare warmed the back of his head. He could see the dark red stretching out from under him, suddenly brighter, and in the center, like a ghost, the vague shadow of the handle, sticking out of his ear.

He tried to think, and all he came up with was that guy in the yellow sweater, waiting for him, here. So here was someone who knew what an ice pick was, after all. Some yuppie kid in a stupid yellow sweater. But still, he managed to do what JK never could.

"Go away," he said again, and the handle jerked, and suddenly he could see through that brick wall, and everything beyond. "Go away. What you see, you can't, un-see, you know?"

But either she didn't hear, or she didn't listen. Where were her fucking parents? Her eyes so big, she'd never forget him. It wasn't right. But there she was, so beautiful over there, and him so ugly over here. Then the handle jerked, and jerked again. And there he was.

ACKNOWLEDGEMENTS

"2PM: The Real Estate Agent Arrives" originally appeared in *Crimewave #10*, 2008

"Saguaro Night" appears here for the first time

"In His Image" originally appeared in *Crimewave #2*, 1999

"The Cough" originally appeared in *365 Scary Stories,* Dziemianowicz, Weinberg, and Greenberg editors, 1998

"You Dreamed It" originally appeared in *Saint Magazine #2,* July 1984

"Rat Catcher" originally appeared in *Dark At Heart,* Joe and Karen Lansdale editors, 1992

"Blood Knot" originally appeared in *Forbidden Acts,* Nancy Collins editor, 1995

"The Carving" originally appeared in *Argosy #3*, 2005

"The Child Killer" originally appeared in *Monsters In Our Midst,* Robert Bloch editor, 1993

"Friday Nights" originally appeared in *Crimewave #8,* 2005

"Squeezer" originally appeared in *New Crimes* #3, Maxim Jakubowski editor, 1991

"Sharp Edges" originally appeared in *Dark Terrors* #3, Steve Jones and David Sutton editors, 1997

"Wet Kisses In The Dark" originally appeared in *Hardboiled #23*, 1997

"The Stench" originally appeared in *Shivers V,* Richard Chizmar editor, 2009

"The Crusher" originally appeared in *Crimewave #6*, 2002

"Living Arrangement" originally appeared in *Crimewave #11,* 2011

"Jesse" originally appeared in *Psycho-Paths,* Robert Bloch editor, 1991

"Stones" originally appeared in *Constable New Crimes #2,* Maxim Jakubowski editor, 1993

"Ugly Behavior" originally appeared in *Out of the Gutter #7,* 2010

18209947R00127

Made in the USA
Lexington, KY
21 October 2012